Y0-CAB-502

Trail to Justice

TRAIL TO JUSTICE

Terrell L. Bowers

AVALON BOOKS
THOMAS BOUREGY AND COMPANY, INC.
NEW YORK

© Copyright 1986 by Terrell L. Bowers
Library of Congress Catalog Card Number: 86-92076
ISBN 0-8034-8630-8

PRINTED IN THE UNITED STATES OF AMERICA
BY HADDON CRAFTSMEN, SCRANTON, PENNSYLVANIA

Trail to Justice

CHAPTER ONE

Spencer Kane stood next to the defendant, who was about to be sentenced.

"Maxwell Pullet," the judge said deliberately, "the jury has found you guilty of the murder of Rupert Clayton, as charged. Do you have anything to say before I sentence you?"

"Wouldn't do me no good, would it?"

"You're entitled to say whatever you wish. Contempt of court could not add to your troubles."

Max looked at Spencer with disdain. "I'm for saying this jackleg lawyer ain't worth the gunpowder it'd take to blow him up! He didn't bust down a single witness against me."

Spence met the heavier man's glare. "Being guilty of murder, you deserved to be tried, not spared punishment."

"See what I mean, Judge? What kind of lawyer did you appoint for me? He wanted to see me hanged all along!"

"Do you have further words, Maxwell Pullet?" the judge asked.

"I done had my say," he grunted.

"The law dictates that you should be hanged. And I sentence you to such punishment on the morrow, May twenty-third, in the year eighteen hundred and seventy-five."

Spence watched as the deputies escorted Max from the courtroom. The few spectators filed out quietly.

"Stick around for a few minutes, Kane," Judge Thomas said to the young lawyer. "I would like to see you in my chambers." Then he walked out of the courtroom, too.

The prosecutor walked over to shake Kane's hand.

"Always a pleasure working against you, Mr. Kane. Not much of a challenge, but always a pleasure."

"One day maybe I'll defend someone who isn't guilty," Spence said. "That could make a difference."

The prosecutor laughed, picked up a handful of papers, and left. Only Spencer Kane remained in the small courtroom, surrounded by silence and emptiness. With a deep sigh, he walked around the judge's bench and entered the chambers of Judge Thomas.

Zack Thomas had removed his robe and was now clad in a regular business suit. He didn't look like the formidable representative of the law who dealt out life or death from his perch. For the first time since Spence had known the man, Zack gave him a smile.

"How about a little brandy? You must be hoarse from defending your client so vociferously."

"I don't find your humor in good taste, but I will have the brandy."

The judge poured both of them a drink and offered Spence a chair. Then Zack sat down behind his desk.

Spence looked at the judge. He couldn't help wondering why Zack Thomas wanted to see him. In nine court appearances before the man, Spence had never won a case.

"You seem to be in a rut, Mr. Kane," the judge said. "It appears that you only get clients who have no chance of winning in court."

"Working in criminal law, I seem to end up with mostly criminals to defend, your honor.

I've not had one innocent man to defend as yet."

"A good lawyer doesn't concern himself with the guilt or innocence of his client. His job is to get him or her off as lightly as possible."

"What good is the law if a fast-talking lawyer can get a guilty person off without paying for his crime?"

"You are not the judge and jury, Kane. It's your job to do what you can for the defendant."

"Max killed that young man, Judge. He picked a fight with a boy half his size and beat him to death with a club. I can't defend someone like that."

The judge took a sip of his drink and leaned back in his chair. He regarded Spence thoughtfully for a time.

"What if you knew your defendant was innocent, Kane? What if the deck had been stacked against him, but there was little evidence on his side? Would you work to get him off then?"

"Certainly. I got into law to see justice was done. That's why I have so much trouble defending the guilty."

"You ever been west of Denver?"

"I've been hunting as far as Fairplay."

"Ever hear of Junction City?"

"Kind of a crossroads town, isn't it?"

"Shipping point for the railroad, nestled in the middle of prime cattle country. There are coal mines, a few ore-producing mines, and a great deal of orchard country in the area."

"What's your point?"

"There is also a sizable population there—three or four thousand people in the valley."

"So?"

"They have an institution in that area, an insane asylum. Are you familiar with such places?"

"Prisons, poorhouses, madhouses. They're all about the same. I've never been inside an asylum, but I've heard some stories."

"There is a climate of reform sweeping through the country, Kane. Until now, no one cared what happened to those unfortunates in an asylum. I've seen some reports that are genuine horror stories, dealing with the filth and degradation those inmates suffer. There are beatings, neglect, starvation, and disease throughout the system. In fact, until recently there have been very few guidelines or laws to govern what goes on in such places."

"Why tell me? I'm a lawyer, not a health inspector."

The judge pulled open a desk drawer and took out an envelope. He removed a soiled letter from it, then read the contents aloud.

"'We urgently request an investigation of the Country Acre Asylum. Cassandra Mattlock is being held a prisoner there so that her rightful estate can be stolen from her. The conditions at that place are terrible, and we fear for the young woman's safety. Please send help at once.'" Judge Thomas looked up from the page. "It's signed by a Mr. and Mrs. Robert Baily, Junction City, Colorado. He's the postmaster there."

Spence felt a tingle of excitement, but there was a churning of apprehension as well. He waited for the judge to continue, trying to remain outwardly calm.

"The governor gave me the letter just yesterday. He asked that I appoint someone to look into the matter. To see the conditions there and make a report. I think you might be the man for that job."

"Me? But I know nothing about asylums," Spence said.

"I have a list of new guidelines that has just been printed. The time for reform has come, but it might reach some areas too late to help some of the present victims. It sounds as if there might be more to this Country Acre Asylum than poor living conditions. You've just told me that you want to uphold the law and see justice done. I'm giving you that chance, Kane."

"I don't know, Judge. What kind of authority will I have?"

"The territorial governor is our highest official in Colorado. You'll carry his seal of approval and the papers I draw up for you. The federal government is also involved."

Spence thought about it for a moment or two. "All right, Judge. I'm your man."

"I'll have the papers ready by tomorrow afternoon. You can start out the next day. There's a train as far as Glenwood Springs. You can catch the stage from there."

Spence packed his clothes and took out his gun and holster. He oiled the gun, then worked the leather with some mink oil. It had been some time since he'd practiced, but he didn't expect to be shooting at anyone in Junction City. All the same, he also took a rifle with him.

After everything was packed, he went down to the sporting club where he usually spent a couple of hours once or twice a week. He exercised and boxed for the enjoyment of it, never fighting out of anger or for money.

Today there was no one around to box with, so he punched the heavy bag. It was good to let his muscles get some action. He could pound away with all his might and not have to think about anything. And that relaxed him, allowing his mind to clear.

After a bath and shave, Spence picked up the promised papers and some printed material from Judge Thomas. A full month's salary was paid in advance, and the judge talked to him for a long time.

In his boardinghouse room that night, Spence looked at the small leaflet that contained the government guidelines for asylums. He also looked at the letter written by the Bailys, which the judge had given him.

So Mr. and Mrs. Baily thought that Cassandra Mattlock had been imprisoned in an insane asylum because someone wanted to steal her property. He didn't like that at all.

Coming from a poor family, Spence knew what it was like to feel vulnerable, helpless. He'd had a hard time working his way through law school after both his parents had died. Many of his classmates thought of him as too ignorant, too unpolished, to ever pass the bar exam and become a practicing lawyer. But he did well in school.

His performance in court was another matter. So far he'd handled fifteen court cases and lost every one of them. A perfect record of sorts. He also had a perfect record in the amateur boxing ring. He'd fought ten fights, winning all of them.

Once again Spence thought of his law-school days. While he was a student, he'd stayed at a boardinghouse run by Nell Bethea, a kindly middle-aged woman who never grew tired of listening to a young man's problems. She provided a shoulder to cry on, and she knew how to keep secrets and how to build up a person's confidence.

As far as Spence knew, she'd never been married, never had children of her own. But she'd been the best kind of mother to the students staying at her boardinghouse.

Spence stared up at the ceiling. "What would you tell me about this trip, Nell? Should I accept the challenge, or am I being a fool? Is this totally out of my line of endeavor? Am I only asking for trouble?"

He pictured the woman's soft features in his mind. He knew that she would smile, gently pat him on the shoulder, and tell him that he was up to the task. He sure hoped that was so.

CHAPTER TWO

It was wash-up day at the Country Acre Asylum. Cassie shivered in her full-length undergarment in dread anticipation. When the water came, she sucked in her breath and tried to block the spray with her arms. The blast of icy liquid was such a shock to her body that she cried out.

Hers was not the only scream. Seven women, eight children, and eleven men were being doused with the freezing water, and most of them were screaming.

The guards laughed and jeered at them. One of the men with a hose purposely aimed it at the old woman everyone simply called "witch." Soon she fell to the slippery floor,

11

knocked down by the pressure of the water.

"All right!" Strummer finally shouted over the noise of the guards. "That will do it for this week. Get the dummies back where they belong."

Strummer was a stocky man, brutal at times, with three missing teeth and no hair on his head. He made Cassie's skin crawl each time he looked at her. Whenever there was reason for a flogging, it was Strummer who wielded the whip.

"Let's go!" one of the guards was shouting. "Get back to your places."

One little girl, who had a monkey-like face and a deformed hand, was sitting on the floor sobbing. Cassie hurried over to pick her up. She was about nine, but her mind was that of a two-year-old. In Cassie's arms, she quieted down, but she still shivered from the cold.

There were three dormitories at the asylum: one for the men, one for the women, and one for the children. Careful not to slip on the puddles of cold, sloppy water, Cassie carried the child from the washing room to the children's dormitory.

"You don't belong down here!" snapped the ill-tempered nurse who looked after the youngest inmates.

"I only brought this child. She's frightened,

wet, and freezing from the cold water."

"Put her down and get back to your own dormitory!" the woman snapped. "Jenny can walk."

"Couldn't you just hold her for—"

"Put her down!" the woman shouted.

Little Jenny began to cry once more, but Cassie put her down on the nearest bed. It was heartbreaking to see the young girl, still in her wet underthings, curl up into a ball, huddling against the chill. Her pained eyes were on Cassie, as if pleading with her.

The nurse suddenly slapped Cassie. "Back to your own section, dummy!" she snapped. "If Strummer has to take you back, you'll spend the rest of the day chained to the wall!"

That made Cassie rush into the women's dormitory, where she tried to dry herself off a little. Then she donned the ragged dress she'd been wearing for over two months. Having nothing to do, she sat down on her bed. The single blanket on her bunk was pulled up around her to fight the chills that always followed the weekly washing.

One woman was lying on her bed. She had been coughing long and hard for more than a month. Her face was red with fever, and she had wasted away to little more than skin and bones. It was a wonder that she'd managed the walk to the room where they were hosed down. From the looks of her, she might never be making that trip again.

Cassie observed the five other women one at a time. All of them had suffered from some kind of craziness—all but the witch. That poor old woman had killed someone's dog and eaten it. It had merely been the desperate act of a starving person. There had been nothing insane about it. But it had been one of Daton Umbridge's dogs. Finding out that the woman had no one to protect her—and that she was dirty, antisocial, and hated children —Umbridge had her sent to the insane asylum. Here she would stay until the day she died.

Ignoring the wails of one of the more vocal women, Cassie remembered how she'd come to be imprisoned in the county institution. She knew there was nothing wrong with her, knew she wasn't crazy. She didn't hear or see things that weren't there. She'd been perfectly all right one minute, then confined in the asylum the next. But she was perfectly sane. It didn't make any sense to her.

Strummer's appearance at the door quieted the noisy woman's lament. In fact, Strummer commanded the tomblike silence whenever he entered a room. Too many had felt his whip or been knocked senseless by his meaty hands. Even though their minds were not working properly, they didn't provoke the man's wrath.

"Exercise in five minutes," he grunted through thick, pasty lips. "Anyone not ready to go out will be chained for the remainder of the day."

"Mr. Strummer," Cassie said timidly, fearfully.

The man's eyes bored into her like hot coals. "What do you want, dummy?"

"Gloria needs attention," she said meekly. "You can see that she's very sick."

The man's eyes flicked over to the coughing woman. "She'll be on the ground in five minutes, or she'll be chained for the day."

"But she's very sick!" Cassie protested. "She needs proper care or she might die!"

He continued to probe Cassie with his burning gaze. "I'll worry about Gloria, dummy. If she dies, it'll be one less of you crowded into this room."

"But that's Gloria Umbridge! That's Daton's wife!"

The man smiled. "Why do you think Daton sent her to us, dummy? He has a yen for Laura Woods. Once Gloria is declared incurably insane, he can get a divorce. If she dies, he'll be free of her even sooner."

"But her sons, Sonny and Aaron. They

can't know about all this! If they find out, they'll help her!"

"Daton owns the ranch. He pulls all the strings in the valley. His sons will side him, no matter what. They haven't so much as visited Gloria since she was sent here six months ago."

"And me? Is that why I'm here? Am I just an inconvenience to Daton and my stepbrother?"

Strummer didn't reply.

"Five minutes!" he called. "Anyone left in the room will be chained to the wall." His eyes found Cassie once more. "Anyone!"

CHAPTER THREE

Spence took a bath and shaved, then put on some clean clothes and went downstairs. He wasn't fond of the derby hat, but he wanted to look professional. His Navy Colt remained in his suitcase.

It didn't take long for Spence to change his mind about the gun, though. On the main street of Junction City, every man seemed to have a revolver on his hip. So Spence returned to the hotel for his own weapon. His frock coat pretty much concealed it, anyway. And something told him he'd be carrying that gun a lot—that he'd also be using his rifle.

Since the Country Acre Asylum was five

miles out of town, he went to the livery to rent himself a horse. The old hostler had nothing on his hands but time and curiosity. He looked Spence over, as if trying to figure out what he was all dressed up for.

"You must be a doctor of some kind. Is that it?"

Spence ignored the question, checking the cinch on the saddle, then adjusting the stirrups.

"You sellin' some kind of medicine? You a drummer?"

"I'd always understood that men out here kept to themselves and didn't ask a lot of questions."

"You don't look like no gunman to me." The hostler grinned. "But is that what you are?"

"Let's just say that I was the boxing champ at my college."

The old man said, "You a college boy, are you?"

"What is it to you what I am? I'm only renting a horse, not moving into your house with you."

"Mighty touchy, ain't you?" the old man grunted. "I'm just a sociable sort. You ain't no nevermind to me. If'n you don't want to shoot the bull together, that's just fine. I kin take a hint."

"I've got business at the Country Acre Asylum. Could you direct me to it?"

"That's the way it is, is it?" the man grumbled. "It's all right for you to put your questions to me, but you bite my head off if'n I ask anything of you."

Spence sighed in defeat. "I'll find it myself."

"Five miles south, on the main road," the old man offered at last. "Big sprawling affair with a high wire fence. You won't miss it."

"Thank you very much. I'll return the horse later today."

"Sure you ain't a doctor of some kind?"

Spence climbed aboard the horse and looked down at the old hostler. "I'm not a doctor. Let's just say I'm visiting someone at the asylum."

"Nope. I doubt it. Them what's admitted don't never come back out. Once a person is crazy, they's crazy. No one don't visit 'em. Don't never get none of them back to normal."

"I've read that sometimes crazy people can return to normal," Spence said. "It happens."

"Not at the Country Acre Asylum, son. Only visitors out there are other doctors or people wanting someone put away. I figured you might be heading out to treat one of the patients that was ailing."

"There supposed to be someone sick?"

"I heard tell that one of the women is in a bad way. The doc at the asylum ain't much good. And the local medico here is an old fellow. He don't get around too good." The hostler paused to look Spence over once more. "Now I take the time to notice, you couldn't be no doctor. You ain't got one of them black bags."

"I don't suppose you know the name of the sick woman?"

"I don't spread rumors, son. What I hear, I keeps private."

"I understand."

"As I recall," the hostler said, scratching his head, "I didn't catch a name. It were Seeton who mentioned it to me. I think he said it was a woman, but I don't remember no name."

"Who's this Seeton?" Spence asked.

"He's one of the attendants at the asylum. He works out there, but he lives in town. I seen him just this morning."

"Thanks."

"You ain't going to work out there, are you?"

"No."

"And you ain't no doctor?"

Spence said, "I'm just going to visit the place."

"You won't get past the front gate," the old man told him smugly. "Ain't no one just visits the asylum."

"I'll get in," Spence said firmly, putting his horse into motion.

"If'n you do," the man called toward his back, "you'll never get out again!"

It took Spence only an hour to reach the place. As the old man had told him, it was surrounded by a high wire fence. The long, white, one-storied building looked grim with bars on the windows and drawn curtains. There was a guard at a steel-barred gate. He watched Spence's approach with wary eyes.

"Good morning," Spence greeted the man.

"What do you want?" the guard asked coldly.

"I'd like to speak to Dr. Vanbough. I was told that he was in charge of this institution."

"He didn't leave word that anyone was coming to visit."

"Perhaps you'd tell him that I'm here."

"Yeah? And who are you?"

Spence calmly said, "Tell him that a representative of the government is here to inspect the premises. Governor Routt has approved my appointment, and I'm to have access to all territory institutions or facilities."

"If Vanbough wants you on the grounds,

you get on. Otherwise, you can sit right where you are till your horse dies of old age."

"Just inform the good doctor that I'm here," Spence said.

The guard checked the lock on the gate, then turned up the long walk toward the front of the building. He moved slowly, as if he had all the time in the world.

Spence dismounted, waiting impatiently for the guard to return.

It was a full fifteen minutes before another man—this one with white hair and a white coat—came to the gate.

"What is it you want?" Dr. Vanbough demanded.

"I've got a letter of introduction from Governor Routt. I'm here to look over the conditions of your establishment."

The white-haired man didn't look very happy. "Who sent you?" he snapped.

"I'm representing both Washington and the Colorado Territory. We're interested in the treatment being given to the insane, the poor, and those who are in prison."

"We don't need your services here," the man said shortly. "You'll have to find someone else to inspect and intimidate."

"As a doctor, sir, you know that I must insist. I have the legal backing to close this institution down unless you cooperate."

"You think so, do you?" Dr. Vanbough was indignant.

"I know so," Spence told him firmly. "Either you allow me to operate freely, or I'll have the local authorities come here to enforce my orders. Let's not make that necessary."

The guard approached the two of them. He stopped next to the white-haired man.

"I passed along your instructions, Dr. Vanbough. You want me to get rid of this pest?"

With a sigh of disgust, Vanbough stepped back from the gate.

"We might as well get this over with. Allow this gentleman to enter."

Spence entered with his horse. The guard took the reins and led the animal to a hitching post. The doctor turned toward the building, so Spence fell in behind him silently.

As they reached the main door, Vanbough stopped. "You said that you had a letter of introduction or somesuch?"

Spence handed him the document from the governor's office.

The doctor looked at it. "Proper Health and Treatment Program." He shook his head in contempt. "This is a bunch of hogwash!"

"Being a doctor, you ought to agree that insane people should get decent care, proper treatment."

"I didn't say that I didn't agree with proper treatment."

"Just object to having someone inspect your work or institution?"

"I don't think the government has any right sticking its big snoot into local institutions and their operations."

"Let's get down to business, Dr. Vanbough. I came here to do my job. It makes no difference to me whether you agree with this inspection or not. I'm here to see your inmates, to see how this place is run, and to make my report to both the territorial governor and to Washington."

The doctor was burning. But he kept his mouth shut and opened the door for Spence.

CHAPTER FOUR

Cassie struggled with Strummer, but the man was too strong for her. He kept her pressed against the wall.

"All you've got to do is take your medicine," he coaxed, holding the small glass next to her mouth.

She struggled some more—in vain. "I don't need any medicine," she told him. "There is nothing wrong with me!"

He grinned. "I agree with you, Cassie. There ain't one blessed thing wrong with you. You're quite a woman. I bet that old boyfriend of yours likely never kissed you like a real man."

"You don't know anything about Jerrod!" she flared. "He was a gentleman!"

"He was a weakling," Strummer said. "He didn't deserve a woman like you. But I think I do."

"You filthy beast!" she cried. "Leave me alone!"

But Strummer didn't leave her alone. He was there to give her her medicine. And he placed a meaty paw over her face, pinching her nose so hard that she had to open her mouth for air. Then he poured the liquid down her throat. She gagged and tried to spit it out, but his free hand was now over her mouth.

"Swallow it!" he commanded. "Swallow it or drown in it!"

Out of breath, half choking on the solution, Cassie swallowed.

Strummer laughed triumphantly, then moved away from her.

"You're a vulgar animal, Strummer," she said tightly. "Someday I hope to see you cut down to size."

"It'll never happen, my sweet Cassandra," he laughed. "There ain't a man in all of Junction City who could take me in a fight."

"What did you make me swallow?"

"Something to help you relax. You've been actin' restless the past couple of days."

"I have not!" she said, sitting down on her bed.

He lifted a careless shoulder. "It don't make no difference, sweet thing. You'll be in dreamland in a couple minutes."

"That's how I got here in the first place, isn't it? I was drugged, and that's why I sounded so crazy at the court hearing. Then I was brought here."

Strummer ignored her words.

"Sleepy-bye time," he chuckled. "See you tomorrow."

The drug was a fast-working compound, and Cassie quickly fell asleep.

The asylum office had been neat and clean. But Spence was soon to discover the rest of the place was dirty, smelly, dismal. He visited the children's dormitory first. The filth was everywhere. The floor hadn't seen a mop or broom in at least a month. The bedding hadn't been changed in ages. Most of the youngsters simply sat on the floor or rocked on their heels, staring absently off into space. Their clothing was soiled and tattered.

Spence didn't say anything about the conditions to Vanbough. But he looked at everything and tried hard to keep it all fixed in his mind.

When they went to the men's ward, Spence

saw there was a deck of cards at the only table, but no one was sitting in the chairs. Most of the men were in the beds or on the floor.

Spence did ask about one man who was chained to the wall and barking like a dog.

The doctor shrugged. "When they start acting wild, we have to do what we can to control them. They usually settle down after a few hours."

There were six sets of chains attached to the wall, Spence noted before he and Vanbough left for the sludge-coated washroom.

"How often do the inmates bathe?" Spence asked.

"We get the town fire wagon here once a week and hose them down. Most of our charges are dirty within hours. These are real lowlifes, Mr. Kane. You can't expect them to act like normal human beings."

"Treat them like animals long enough, and they'll become animals, Doctor. If you ask me, being hosed down with cold water is more of a punishment than a method of cleaning."

"We haven't got the staff to attend to each of them personally. The small grant from Junction City and a few of the farmers and ranchers barely puts food on the table for them."

Spence dropped the debate, and soon the two men entered the women's ward, which was as dirty and depressing as the rest of the institution. Here there were also six sets of chains attached to the wall. Some of the women were talking gibberish. Some were silent.

Turning his head, Spence saw a bed that was occupied by a woman in her forties. It wasn't until he walked closer to her that he realized how thin and pale she was, and how hard she had to gasp for each breath. She seemed to be on the verge of death.

"What happened to this woman?"

"She became ill a few weeks ago. Pneumonia set in. She probably won't live out the week."

"What are you doing for her?" Spence asked.

The doctor's face grew dark. "Are you a qualified physican?"

"No."

"Then you couldn't possibly know that we're doing all we can for this woman. She's given special medication, fed three times a day, and constantly made comfortable. With pneumonia, there is little more we can do for her. She would get no better treatment in our hospital in Junction City!"

"What's her name?" Spence asked.

"Gloria Umbridge. She used to be queen of the entire valley until she suffered a mental collapse."

Spence looked around at the other women once more. He spotted one in a corner, sound asleep. The doctor tried to block Spence's path as he started to walk toward that particular woman.

"Must you trouble these wretched creatures? You'll only upset them!" Vanbough said.

Spence stepped around him, continuing to cross the room. He stopped at the young woman's bed and looked down at her. She was the most attractive of the lot. Her blond hair was combed, and she was cleaner than the others. She slept very soundly, almost in an unnatural slumber.

"Who is this one?"

"Her name is Cassandra Mattlock. She's been with us for about three months."

"What seems to be wrong with her?" Spence asked.

"She's insane, thinks everyone is against her. She can't sleep without the aid of drugs."

Spence lifted her hand, then slapped it lightly, but he got no response. He felt her forehead and lifted one eyelid. The girl was lost to the world, completely limp and unaware of her surroundings.

Gently placing the hand back at her side, Spence turned to the doctor once more. He didn't like the narrow, suspicious look in Vanbough's eyes. Here was a weasel, a crafty, underhanded sneak of a man. He had the label of doctor, but that didn't mean he really knew what he was doing.

"I will select several people to speak to in private. It's part of my inspection," Spence said.

"And if I refuse?"

"I'll get a court order to close this place down," he said simply. "I have the authority to do that, you know."

"You're a real troublemaker, aren't you?" the doctor said.

"Will you comply, or do I visit the judge and marshal in town?"

With a great deal of effort, the older man appeared to compose himself. "Which inmates do you wish to see?"

"The old woman there, and the girl who's sleeping in the corner. I'll pick two men and one of the children as well."

"And when do you intend to speak to them?"

"Tomorrow."

"Very well, Mr. Kane. Shall we return to the men's quarters?"

"Certainly," Spence agreed, surprised that

the man was giving in so easily. "I'll choose the three others that I need to interview."

"We'll have them dressed and ready for you tomorrow," Vanbough said tightly. "I'm sure you'll find that we treat our inmates here with the utmost of care and attention."

Spence felt a warning bell go off in his head, but he ignored it. He had pushed as much as he dared for one day. That the doctor was going to let him speak privately with several people was more than he'd dared hope. He didn't actually have much power. He'd bluffed his way through, not really knowing if he could have gotten a judge to close the asylum. It was a good thing the doctor had decided to cooperate.

CHAPTER FIVE

It was early afternoon when Spence entered the Junction City combination post office and general store.

He was forced to browse for a time, waiting for the store's three customers to leave. Once he had the place to himself, he confronted the elderly man behind the counter.

"I'm looking for the Bailys. Would you be Robert?"

"Everyone calls me Bob, but that's me all right. What can I do for you?"

"I represent the governor and a special branch of the territorial government. I'm here in response to your letter concerning the Country Acre Asylum."

The man looked around quickly, a frightened expression crossing his face. He took a few steps around the counter, grabbed Spence's arm, and took him to the back of the store. He didn't stop until they were in the hall that led to the Bailys' private quarters at the rear of the house.

"Best keep our names out of this, son," the man said in a hushed voice. "Daton wouldn't take kindly to us siding against him."

"Daton?"

"Daton Umbridge. He owns twelve thousand acres and has access to twice that much more. He owns the second biggest ranch in Colorado. Part of his holdings are what used to belong to Cassandra Mattlock."

"I need to talk to you about that. When can we get together?"

"Slip around to the back door after dark. Make sure that no one sees you. I don't want to end up in that madhouse."

"Daton is that powerful?'" Spence asked.

"On the west side of the Rockies, the big man is Daton Umbridge. He has nearly a hundred men on his payroll, and some of his hands are known for their skill with a gun."

"I'll remember," Spence told Baily as they walked back to the store. "See you after dark."

Bob Baily looked out the store window.

"You're already in trouble, son. That man out there is called Strummer, and he works over at the Country Acre Asylum. I'd say that you've already ruffled some feathers."

Spence looked out at the man. He wore no hat, revealing a smooth, bald head. He was standing there like a stumpy tree, hands on his hips, his jaw outthrust, his eyes searching the interior of the store. There could be little doubt who he was looking for—or why.

Baily said, "You can get out the back of the house. Maybe you ought to avoid Strummer. He's a vicious man in any kind of a fight."

"I'm not altogether without boxing skills," Spence told the older man tightly. "And my folks didn't raise any cowards in the family. If Strummer is looking for me, I won't disappoint him."

"He won't fight fair if you start getting the best of him," Baily warned.

"There's only one way to fight, Mr. Baily, and that is to win!"

Strummer's eyes flashed as Spence came out on the sidewalk. There were already a few people gathering. Strummer was a man who liked an audience.

"You must be Kane," he said. "You've been bothering our patients. I don't like them being disturbed."

"From what I hear," Spence said easily,

"you're the one that's disturbed. Perhaps you're the one who should be locked up in the asylum."

The man's fists knotted, his arms thick and powerful. He was a few inches shorter than Spence, but he must have weighed thirty pounds more.

"Step down from that walk, city slicker. I'm going to teach you a lesson in humility. I aim to tear your head off!"

Spence took a moment to shrug out of his frock coat. He folded it neatly and laid it on a bench in front of the store. The crowd was gathering now, like flies drawn to a bloated carcass.

"Come on, you meddling dude!" Strummer growled. "Come and get a taste of my knuckles!"

"Are you sure we can't settle this without violence?" Spence asked.

"Only if you were to turn and run," Strummer grated. "There's a stage leaving town in an hour. You can get on it yourself, or I'll beat you to a pulp and throw you on it!"

Spence shook his shoulders, loosening his muscles, and ducked or blocked Strummer's first few punches. When he hit Strummer solidly in the nose, the crowd roared. The two fighters circled, Strummer still trying desperately to hit Spence, who continued to duck and block, to counter with a left jab that had been developed over long hours of practice.

Strummer had received several bad blows before he succeeded in punching Spence a few times. His early blows did very little damage, though. As the battle went on, Spence continued to outmaneuver the heavier brawler at every turn.

Despite a swollen eye and many cuts and bruises, Strummer kept fighting, fueled by a fury that demanded the newcomer's blood. Soon he made his opponent feel the pain of his angry fists. But he simply couldn't defeat Spence. And when Strummer fell to the ground, dazed and battered to a pulp, the onlookers cheered again.

I'll get even with him, Strummer vowed before he lost consciousness. If it's the last thing I do, I'll make that dude sorry he was ever born.

CHAPTER SIX

It was an hour past full dark before Spence made his way carefully around to the rear of the combination general store and post office. He knocked on the door softly, and it was soon opened by an elderly woman.

"Come in, Mr. Kane," she said, offering him a smile of greeting.

Spence stepped in, removing his hat, waiting for her to close the door behind him.

"This way," she said, leading him through a narrow kitchen and into a small but comfortable-looking parlor.

Bob Baily had a pipe lit. He was sitting in a leather chair, his stocking feet propped up on a stool. As his wife left the room, he nodded toward the sofa against the wall.

"Sit down, Mr. Kane. I'm sure you must be quite worn out after that bit of exercise this afternoon. You paid back a lot of debts today. I can't think of anyone in town that Strummer hasn't bullied at one time or another. I must say you took him apart like a paper hat."

"I'm glad it looked that way, but he gave me all I wanted and more. I'm going to be too stiff to walk comfortably tomorrow."

"My missus is going to bring us some coffee. Smoke if you like."

"I'm not a smoking man," Spence said.

"I hear tell you only took one free drink, too."

"It helped with the soreness in my mouth. That's the only reason I took it."

"A government man with no vices," Baily grinned. "I never figured to meet one of those in my lifetime."

"Depends on what you call vices. I happen to be sticking my nose into other people's affairs here in Junction City. If I get it snipped off, I'll have learned a real serious lesson in minding my own business."

"Speaking of that business," Bob said, "what have you found out about the asylum?"

"A place like that could drive anyone out of his mind. Those inmates live in surroundings that aren't much better than a stable. Crazy or not, nobody should be forced to live that way."

"Did you see Cassie?"

Spence sighed. "You mean Cassandra Mattlock? Yes, I saw her."

"How'd the poor girl look?"

At that moment Mrs. Baily returned to the room with cups of coffee. After putting both cream and sugar in Spence's, she handed it to him.

"Thank you, ma'am."

"You were talking about Cassie?" she said anxiously.

"She was drugged. I tried to speak to her, but she was dead to the world. I'm supposed to see her tomorrow, and she'd better not be drugged then."

"That's the way they most likely got her in there. By drugging her. I'd bet my upper teeth on it!" Bob declared. "First thing you know, that Daton Umbridge will own this whole valley and everyone in it!"

"Can you back up a little?" Spence said. "I saw a woman near death in the asylum. Someone said her name was Gloria Umbridge. Now what's the whole story on them?"

The old couple exchanged glances.

Then Bob sipped his coffee and said,

"Daton came into the valley right after the Utes were signed to a treaty and moved away from the area. He put men on homesteads, filed on every bit of land he could lay his hands on, and came to control several thousand acres.

"Joe Mattlock owned a fair-sized piece of land over toward the desert. He had a thousand head of cattle, several hands, and a nice home. He also had Cassie and a stepson, Alvin Peek, who never changed his name.

"Things looked pretty good for the Mattlocks. Cassie was seeing a lot of the coal-mine owner named Jerrod Steel, and Joe was even courting a local widow. His wife had died several years back. As for Alvin, he was never worth the powder it would take to blow him away. He spent money recklessly, ran up bills all over town, and he was even thrown in jail a time or two.

"Then about three months back, some rustlers were probably seen on the Mattlock spread." Bob narrowed his eyes. "At least, that's the way the story goes. Joe and Jerrod were together, possibly discussing Cassie's future. It looks like they stumbled onto some men branding calves, and there was a gunfight. When the smoke cleared away, Joe Mattlock and Jerrod Steel were both dead."

"Any trace of the rustlers?" Spence asked.

"One of the calves was found with part of a brand, but it wasn't finished. There was no way to even tell what the brand would have been. Anyhow, people naturally figure that Joe and Jerrod were shot by rustlers."

"And no one saw these rustlers?"

"Nary a track or trace," Bob grunted. "Next thing we hear, Cassie is supposed to have lost her mind—gone crazy—after the death of both her pa and her fiance. That puts the reins of the Mattlock spread directly into Alvin's hands."

"Let me guess what comes next. Alvin is selling out to Umbridge," Spence said.

"The sale was made last month. Daton now owns the Mattlock ranch and all of the cattle with it. Cassie doesn't get a dime of her rightful inheritance because she's been declared legally insane."

"Very neat," Spence said.

"That sleazy runt, Alvin, should be hung from the nearest tree. He was in on the killing as sure as you're sitting across from me now."

"That might take some doing to prove."

"Ain't no way to prove a thing, not with Daton holding the entire valley in the palm of his hand."

"What about his wife?" Spence asked.

"She got to be in his way," Bob said with

open disgust. "He grew real fond of a woman in town. The only way to be rid of his wife was to declare her also insane. She'll die in that rotten place."

"After seeing her today, I'd say she doesn't have much longer. That will free him to marry his new love."

"And his boys don't give one hoot about it!" Bob said bitterly. "What kind of scum did that woman raise? Her own boys sit back and let their pa ramrod her right into a death bed, and they do nothing about it!"

"Daton has sons?" Spence asked.

"Two of them, Sonny and Aaron. They're about as worthless as can be. Never seen either of them do a day's work."

"What else can you tell me about the asylum?"

"Not much," Bob admitted. "It came into existence five years ago, mostly as a poorhouse. After the first year, it supposedly no longer took the poor, only crazy people. But that's not really true. We've seen a number of old people being sent there, those that were too feeble to get around. Soon after, there would be a funeral for them. Most of them didn't last very long in that place."

"And no one's ever complained or asked for an investigation?" Spence said.

"Most of those sent there are without

money or friends. Even the children there are unwanted and abandoned. No one who loved their child could send them to such a horrid place."

Spence put his cup down on a nearby table. "Does the law belong to Daton?"

"He controls most of what goes on, Kane. You can't expect much help from the marshal, and the judge gets most of his pay directly from the Umbridge ranch. He won't openly do anything dishonest. But he'd never fight Umbridge either."

Spence shook his head. "I believe I've come to a river that's too wide to jump, too fast to swim, and too deep to wade. What little authority I have, it isn't enough to stand up against a judge in court. If I can't get some support, I won't get anything done." Of course, he knew he was only supposed to write a report for the governor and make a copy for the U.S. government. But he ached to do more than that. Spence wanted to help the inmates of that asylum himself, and as quickly as possible.

"What about Cassie?" Mrs. Baily asked. "She doesn't belong in the horrible place!"

Spence said, "There's a chance that Daton won't expect her to stay there. After all, he has her ranch now. He might consider her to be harmless against him now."

"Then you'll help her?"

"I'm supposed to speak to her tomorrow. I hope we'll be able to do something for her."

"We'll be thankful for anything you can do," Mrs. Baily said softly. "We've known Cassie since she was a child. She wasn't the kind of girl to go to pieces—not even after such a terrible shock. She loved her father, sure, and I think she was quite fond of Jerrod. But I don't believe she went crazy when they died."

Spence spent another hour with the Bailys. They were sincere about wanting to help, but they were also very frightened of Daton Umbridge. That much was clear.

Returning to the hotel, Spence slipped quietly into his room. He had a lot of thinking to do, a lot of planning.

He didn't know what to expect the next day or the days after that. It seemed like a good idea to practice drawing his Navy Colt, though. Just in case.

So practice he did. But Spence had a long, long way to go before he was half as good with a gun as he was with his fists.

CHAPTER SEVEN

Cassie felt weak from sleeping for almost twenty-four hours. She followed Seeton down the hall wordlessly, wondering what was going on. She had heard broken whispers among the other inmates about a visitor, but it meant nothing to her.

Alvin, who had signed the papers to commit her, would not be visiting her. The few friends she had were not the kind to oppose Daton Umbridge, so she couldn't imagine anyone coming to see her personally.

Seeton led her into a small room. He was another bully, just as bad as Strummer.

"You're to change clothes and wait here for Dr. Vanbough," he growled.

Cassie saw that a white dress had been laid out for her, with matching stockings and shoes. There was also a hairbrush and small hand mirror.

"There's water in the pan, and a cloth and towel," Seeton said.

She gave him a questioning look. "What is all this for?"

"Just do what you're told," he snapped. "If you can't do it by yourself, I'll help you get out of your clothes!"

"I can manage," she said quickly.

"You've got about ten minutes. Be ready."

Cassie was relieved to see the man turn for the door.

After washing herself as best she could, she hurriedly dressed, then brushed her hair. She hadn't worn anything clean for so long that she felt incredibly spoiled. She went so far as to spin around lightly, allowing the dress to swirl. It was a fairly good fit, and she could actually feel human wearing it.

The door opened to subdue her spirits. Dr. Vanbough entered and looked Cassie over carefully from head to foot. When his lifeless blue eyes rested on her face, she cringed.

"You'll be talking to a government representative in a few minutes, Miss Mattlock," the doctor said guardedly. "I expect you to sit through the interview without offering the man a word. If you decide to talk to him, I'll see that your stay with us becomes a nightmare."

She swallowed, thinking of Strummer's whip, of the very dark, very small, very damp cages that were located underground. Cages that were visited only by insects, mice, and rats.

"I see from the look on your face that you know it's wise to cooperate with us. Remember this, Cassandra, no matter what this man tells you, no matter what his promises, you are lawfully committed to stay with us. A legal hearing would take a month or more, and there would be a long waiting period before you would be released—even if you were found sane. Before you managed to get out of here, anything might happen."

Cassie asked, "But why do this to me? My ranch is lost, Alvin has his blood money, and Daton can't be afraid of me. Why must you keep me here?"

"You just do as I tell you, Miss Mattlock. If you open your mouth to this man, I'll see you spend the next few weeks in hell!"

Cassie sat down in one of the two chairs in the room. Her spirits were crushed, her hopes dashed. Dr. Vanbough would keep his promise, and she would never be free.

* * *

Spence got nothing out of the two men. One had been tortured by a couple of Ute Indians who had discovered that he had been cheating them. The Indians loved to gamble, but they were hard on cheaters, and the man's experience with them had left him insane, sobbing and talking nonsense. Spence knew nothing about the second man, but he too seemed totally out of his head. He constantly hummed to himself, a mindless tune that was enough to drive a sane man to the madhouse.

The little girl, who was eight or nine, could barely utter a few one-syllable words. After some prompting, she told Spence that she wished she had a doll to play with. Her speech was hard to understand, and it took a lot of coaxing, but he felt that this child could be loving and warm, even if her mind never matured, even if she thought like a three-year-old for the rest of her life.

Lastly, Spence went to see the two women. He chose to speak to the woman known as the witch first. It was a waste of time, for she never uttered a single word. It was as if she'd been warned not to speak to him. He couldn't get her to try the chocolate or sugar sticks he'd brought with him. She seemed frightened and wouldn't even take a drink of the fresh coffee.

She was as firm as granite, keeping a stone mask for a face, ignoring everything Spence said. The only time she looked at him was at the start of their session, as if deciding that he wasn't worth the effort. With that defeat, he was left only with Cassie.

It was a pleasant surprise to see Cassandra Mattlock, for she looked very nice in a gown of white. A glance at her big gray eyes told Spence that she was alert, intelligent, and probably quite normal. But the old woman had seemed normal, too. Also—like the old woman—Cassie had a scared look, as if she'd been warned to keep quiet.

"Good morning, Miss Mattlock," he said cheerfully. "I'm glad to see that you're awake and up and about."

She silently peered at the floor, clasping her hands in front of her. She looked very innocent, very demure in such a pose.

"I'm a representative of the federal government and the governor of the territory. We're interested in the humane treatment of people in institutions across the country. I also happen to be a lawyer, though I haven't had much success in that field as yet."

His words might just as well have been aimed at the wall. If the girl was even listening to him, it wasn't apparent.

"I've visited with some of the other inmates," Spence went on in a matter-of-fact voice. "Are some of them friends of yours?"

She didn't respond or look up.

"A little while ago, I met a sweet young girl by the name of Jenny. It's a shame that her parents didn't want to keep her. Do you know her?"

Cassie raised her eyes for a fleeting moment, regarding him with an odd sort of look. When he offered her a warm, friendly smile, she again lowered her gaze, her lids hiding her sparkling eyes.

"Would you like some coffee?" he asked.

Cassie shook her head negatively.

"I've got some sugar sticks. I gave one to Jenny. I imagine sweets are in rather short supply here. Would you like one?"

Again she shook her head no.

Spence sighed deeply. "Miss Mattlock, I came here to help you. Someone cared enough about you to write to the governor in Denver. I was sent here to look into your plight, as well as examine the goings-on in this institution. Why won't you help me?"

Cassie's gray eyes were lifted to him once more. She opened her mouth a trifle, as if she might speak. But she held back.

"What is it?" Spence coaxed. "Tell me, Cassie!"

She remained silent.

"I can't do a blessed thing if you won't co-operate," Spence said. "If you've been threatened, I'll cover for you. I'll find a way to get you out of here right away. Trust me, Cassie!"

The girl's chest was rising and falling, as if she'd just run a long distance. But she held her silence.

"All right!" Spence snapped angrily. "I've come over two hundred miles to help you, but it's obvious that you don't want any help. I hope you truly enjoy the surroundings you're living in, for you're going to face them for the rest of your life!"

That made her eyes widen.

"That's right, Miss Mattlock," he went on. "You are considered incurably insane. This is to be your permanent residence!"

She shook her head violently. "No!" she gasped. "That can't be!"

"It's true," he said. "You will never leave this place—never!"

She was shaken, uncertain, confused. Her lips parted, but again there were no words.

"I'm your only chance, Cassie!" Spence warned. "Either you confide in me—here and now—or you'll rot here for the rest of your life!"

The girl was torn, wringing her hands, thinking so hard that Spence could almost see the wheels of her mind turning. He had to force her to speak, to make things so clear that she couldn't possibly remain silent.

"See these hands?" he told her, lifting his bruised knuckles. "Strummer was turned lose on me yesterday. These people don't want me around." His jaw became tight. "But I'm still here. If you see Strummer today, he'll look as if he'd been kicked in the face by a horse. I beat him yesterday, and I can beat the doctor here in court. If you'll help me, we'll have you out of here by the end of the week!" Spence meant to do that, too, even though he had not been given the authority.

"Y-you beat Strummer?" the girl asked in a very timid voice.

"I'm not the helpless individual that I appear to be, Miss Mattlock. I will do what I tell you I can do." He stepped closer to her. "You've got to trust me, Cassie. The rest of your life depends on it."

"I . . . I . . ." But she didn't continue.

"I'm going to walk out that door," he threatened. "Once I leave, I'll not be back. If you want my help, you'll have to ask for it. Otherwise, you'll end up just like Gloria Umbridge—dying here!"

Spence hated being so harsh, but soft words hadn't worked. He turned slowly away from the girl, stepping toward the door.

"Please," the girl whispered. "Please, help me."

CHAPTER EIGHT

Judge Olsen Clott lived in a fair-sized house at the edge of town. He held court at the town hall, but he often married couples right in his own home. He had a wife, two grown children who had moved away, a housekeeper, and a noisy little mutt of a dog.

The latter two greeted Spence upon his approach to the house. The dog yipped mightily, as if he thought the sound of his high-pitched bark would frighten away any intruders. The housekeeper was beating a rug, having draped it over the hitching post in the front yard. She was a heavyset woman with unkempt hair and a soiled, worn dress.

Spence removed his hat as he stopped a few

feet away from her. He offered her a smile, but her dull expression told him that she wasn't the cordial sort.

"Good morning, ma'am," he said cheerfully. "Would the judge be in today?"

"He's in," she grunted.

"Do I need to be announced, or should I simply knock?"

"I ain't no doorman," she said. "You'll find the judge sacked out on the couch. Tough night at the bars last night."

"Thank you, ma'am," Spence said, then walked into the house.

He found the paunchy judge in the parlor, sprawled out on an old but comfortable-looking couch. He had one arm over his eyes, his mouth open in slumber, his shoes off, with an empty bottle sitting on the floor. Evidently, Judge Clott enjoyed his drinking.

"Wake up!" Spence snapped. "On your feet, Judge!"

The man groggily opened his eyes.

"Judge Clott, you're a disgrace to the robe!" Spence growled.

The man raised his head now, peering up at Spence. He licked his lips, then rose to his feet on wobbly legs.

"Who are you?"

"I represent the governor and the federal government, Clott," Spence told him with an air of authority. "I'm here to investigate the goings-on in your fair town." He looked the judge over. "I can see why they sent me here. You're nothing but an inebriated shell of a man!"

"Wait a minute!" the judge said, sparks igniting his fogged eyes. "Who are you, and what are you doing in my house?"

"You're in trouble, Clott," Spence went on. "I don't know whether you'll be dismissed or not, but things certainly don't look good for you."

"What?" the judge gasped.

"Colorado has applied for statehood, Clott. The governor and the federal government are conducting investigations, making inquiries, checking the trouble spots in this territory. I'm here to look into some allegations about the Country Acre Asylum."

The judge was still in a haze.

"I want to see the papers connected with the asylum," Spence continued. "I want to see everything pertaining to the commitment of Gloria Umbridge and Cassandra Mattlock."

"I don't know about—"

"If you cooperate, Clott," Spence said, "I might review you more favorably in my report to the President of the United States. If I have to wire for authority to confiscate your records, I won't be so easy to get along with."

The judge was fully alert now. "You look a mite young to be empowered by the territory or federal government to do much of anything."

"You can wire Judge Zachary Thomas over in Denver, and he'll tell you that I have a perfect record in court. Fifteen decisions, and always the same verdict. As you probably know from experience, it doesn't take too much success before a man gets noticed. I was handpicked for this assignment."

"Yes, but—"

"Here is a letter from John Routt, the territorial governor. Perhaps you wish to go against his personal request."

The man glanced at the letter and handed it back. "It doesn't say anything about you getting into my court records."

Spence quoted a federal law that gave him the right to look at the judge's records—and this time he wasn't bluffing.

The judge frowned. "I never read about any such law."

"How long since you studied law, Clott?" Spence said smugly.

"I keep up with new legislation as best I can," the judge said a bit lamely. "We're a long way from Washington."

"Clott, this law was passed five years ago. You should know it. I'd hate to waste time wiring Governor Routt. Do I make my position clear?"

"All right, all right," the judge said reluctantly. "Just what records do you wish to see?"

Within the confines of the dark, damp cage, Cassie huddled in the single blanket. The floor was hard clay. There wasn't enough space for standing or lying down. Endless hours passed, with Cassie forced to remain in a sitting position. A huge rat scurried past her, attracted by the piece of moldy bread she'd been given to eat.

Vanbough had not gotten any confession out of her, but he'd accused her of talking to the lawyer, Spencer Kane. It might have been the fact that they were together for a full fifteen minutes that had alerted him. Or perhaps Kane had said something to give away the fact that she'd broken her silence. Whatever it was, she'd been stuck back into her rags and hustled down to a horrible basement cage.

A light flared, blinding Cassie momentarily. She blinked at the approach of Seeton. He had the key to her cage. He didn't speak but proceeded to unlock her door.

"Come on out, dummy!" he snapped. "Be quick about it!"

Cassie tried, but her legs were stiff, the muscles refusing to obey after many hours in the cell.

Seeton yanked her arm. "Get a move on!" he growled.

Cassie staggered to her feet.

"Move!" He was snarling like a mad dog.

Cassie's muscles responded this time. She hurried to the ladder that would lead her out of the pit.

Dr. Vanbough was waiting for her at the top of the ladder. He grabbed her arm roughly, his fingers biting into the soft flesh.

"What did you tell that lawyer?" he demanded.

Cassie shook her head. "Nothing."

The doctor slapped her face very hard. "Get cleaned up—right now!" he shouted. "I want you dressed and in my office in five minutes!"

Seeton gave her a push toward the women's ward, so she couldn't see where the doctor was going.

"You've done it now, dummy," the attendant sneered. "When we get you back, you'll find that hell would be better than your life. I'll see to that personally!"

Cassie hurried down the hall, her heart pounding. Kane had done it! He was getting her out!

CHAPTER NINE

Spence could see the doctor boiling beneath the surface. His authority had been usurped, his competence questioned, his private domain invaded. Spence had handed him the court order and given him ten minutes to produce the inmate he requested.

It was a dangerous idea, taking the girl away from the asylum, but Spence had made a promise. He knew she didn't belong behind walls, but proving it would be something else again. He wondered if Judge Thomas would approve of his handling of the situation. He was certainly doing a lot of bluffing, but it seemed absolutely necessary.

Vanbough again looked at the order signed

by Judge Clott. "When is this hearing to take place?"

"In two weeks," Spence said.

"And you have custody of my patient till then?"

"That is correct. We'll need time to review the facts, to examine the grounds surrounding Miss Mattlock's commitment. There will be an impartial judge sent from Denver to make a ruling. The matter of Mrs. Umbridge might also arise. How is she doing?"

"You'll never get any testimony from her, Mr. Jackleg Lawyer," the doctor said. "She died last night."

"Very convenient for Daton and his new love, wouldn't you say?"

"I don't know what you mean by that."

"Have you informed the Umbridge clan of Gloria's death?"

"Not yet."

"I'm sure that it'll come as a real surprise. I see from your visitors' record that not one of them has been down to see her the entire length of time she's been here."

"Who told you that you could go snooping through my records?" the doctor demanded indignantly.

"I'm a curious fellow," Spence grinned. "I had to do something while I was awaiting your return."

"You're digging a deep hole for yourself, Kane. I wonder if it isn't going to be so deep that you can't get back out."

"Maybe you'll have a competency hearing on me, Vanbough. I imagine you could even make me look crazy."

"Your being here and interfering already proves that," the doctor said flatly. "If I were you, I'd take the first stage heading east and not look back."

"That might also be sound advice for you, Vanbough. If I can convince a judge of the atrocities you've committed here—in the name of treating the insane—I'll have this place closed down. With luck, I'll even have you in jail facing charges."

"You talk real big, Kane. But you'd better watch yourself real close. A man like you could easily have a bad—maybe even fatal—accident!"

The door opened before Spence could reply to that. He gave a welcoming smile to a very uncertain, hesitant Cassie Mattlock.

"Come in," he said.

"Yes," the doctor grumbled, "come in, Miss Mattlock."

Cassie entered the room timidly, then closed the door behind her. She was again wearing the pretty white dress.

"Inform the patient of the turn of events,"

Spence prodded the white-haired doctor.

Vanbough glared at Spence, then forced the words out. "This man has a court order placing you in his custody, Miss Mattlock. You'll have a new competency hearing in two weeks. I hope you fare adequately in the outside world, but we shall keep a place open for you here—just in case."

Spence took the girl's hand and headed for the door. She came willingly, not offering a word.

Spence led her out of the large building, helped her up into the carriage he'd rented, then went around to climb in next to her.

The guard at the gate glowered at both of them, but he allowed them to pass.

"I kept my promise," Spence said quietly on the way to Junction City.

He was totally unprepared for the girl's response, for she briefly threw her arms around him. Then she sobbed like a child.

"It's all right, Cassie," he told her softly, tenderly. "Let it out if you want. I understand."

"Y-you don't know what it's like," she sniffed. "Never able to relax, never able to forget the misery and horror around you. The wailing, the sounds of people in chains, the beatings, the moldy food. It's a nightmare."

"I've learned as much, Miss Mattlock,"

Spence said. "Before I came here I learned some rather vivid details of life in an asylum. Changes are being made, though, laws drawn up to protect the inmates. But it takes time."

The girl's gray eyes came up to meet his. "W-will I have to go back there?"

He gave her a reassuring smile. "Not if I can help it. I don't think you belong in such a place."

"I don't think anyone belongs there," the girl replied. "Even Jenny, who has the mind of a tiny child, she deserves more."

"First things first," he said. "I'll get you someplace safe, then start rounding up information and evidence for the hearing."

"That'll be dangerous, Mr. Kane. Daton Umbridge is the main supporter of the asylum. He won't like anyone snooping into his affairs."

"I can't help what he likes. I'll do my job."

"You're a very brave man."

"I've never thought much about being brave," he sighed. "A person just has to do what he has to do. Each job has its own challenges. Daton Umbridge will just be one of mine."

She shook her head in a skeptical way. "I should tell you that you are crazy, that you belong in the Country Acre Asylum. I should point out that Daton has a dozen killers on his payroll, that Judge Clott will oppose everything you try to do. I should, but I won't."

"No?"

"You showed that you have some special skills. You beat Strummer in a fight. You got me out of that place. So it's obvious you can perform miracles!"

He laughed. "Let's get you settled. Do you have any belongings stashed anywhere?"

"Alvin sold the ranch, so I imagine everything is gone. I don't know what he'd have done with my clothing and personal things, but I'll probably never see them again."

"The Bailys' home has an attic that is only used for storing things. At my request, they've made room for you to stay there."

"I hate to impose on them. Isn't there—"

"Bob and Emma were quite insistent, Cassie. Besides that, no one is going to know where you are staying. We'll slip you into their house after dark."

"I have to hide out then?"

Spence sighed. "Sorry, Cassie, but it's necessary for the time being. We can't be certain that Daton or Vanbough wouldn't do something rash. I don't want you getting hurt."

She smiled. "No one has been very worried about that lately. But then I haven't worried about—haven't loved—anyone either."

"What about Jerrod Steel?"

"Jerrod was fifteen years older than me, Mr. Kane. I had been seeing him, but it was mostly arranged by my father. I liked Jerrod, and I'm very sorry that he was killed. But I didn't love the man."

"And it made no difference to your father?"

"A girl should marry the man her father chooses. He is looking out only for her interests. That's what Pa kept telling me."

"I suppose a good many fathers are like that. But I've met a few who are much worse. They'd use their daughters to barter with."

"Not my father. He was seeking a partner for me who would take good care of me, who would be a good provider for a family."

"What do you think about the rustling on his ranch?"

"I think my father was purposely killed. Jerrod might have been murdered also to keep anyone from questioning any actions that were to be taken against me."

"And you suspect Daton of being behind it?"

"I don't know. It could have been Alvin, too. He never wanted the ranch life, but that was all he had to look forward to. With the death of my father, then having me committed, he was free to sell the place to Daton and get out."

"I'm told that Alvin has left the country already."

"How much did he get out of the ranch?"

"No one seems to know that. You can bet that it wasn't a great deal. I haven't seen the sale or title papers, but I intend to."

"That could be risky business."

"As your attorney, I have a sworn duty to serve you to the best of my capabilities, Cassie. I'll avoid starting any kind of a fight, but we have the right to know what took place."

"It frightens me," she said quietly. "If anything happens to you, I'll end up back in that awful place."

"For both our sakes, I'll try to see that nothing happens to me, Cassie."

She smiled. "It's settled then. You'll be careful for both our sakes."

CHAPTER TEN

The D Ranch sat at one end of the valley, nestled against some rising mountains, with one side open toward the plains. There were corrals, bunkhouses, barns, and numerous other outbuildings surrounding the elegant three-storied main house.

As Spence rode up to the handsome white mansion, two dogs set up a racket. But someone's firm voice silenced them at once. The voice came from the shadows within the house, but Spence could guess at the owner.

By the time he reached the porch, Daton Umbridge was standing outside.

Stopping the horse, Spence looked down at the tall, muscular man.

71

"You're the snoop from Washington," Daton said.

"I'm from Denver," Spence corrected.

"Denver, Washington. What difference does it make? What do they care about us?"

"Colorado might be a state one day soon."

"And you are the one trying to remake the world?"

Spence looked around slowly. "Seems that I heard the same thing about you. People who get in your way are sent to the Country Acre Asylum and not heard from again."

"Is that what you believe?"

"Yes."

"Then why have you ridden out to see me? You've obviously got something in mind, or else you wouldn't have taken the trouble to get Miss Mattlock released."

Spence looked the man over, not liking him one bit. He was arrogant, smug, drunk with the power he held in the valley. He'd forgotten how to be human.

"I aim to prove that you swindled Miss Mattlock out of her property. Further, I may also prove that you had her father and Jerrod Steel killed."

The man laughed. "That's absurd. It was rustlers who killed Joe Mattlock and Jerrod Steel. Everyone knows about that."

"Hardly a person believes it," Spence countered. "All I need is one witness, one carelessly spoken word. A man like you wouldn't do well in prison."

"There isn't a man in this territory who would even dare to try and put me behind bars, Mr. Kane. I suggest that you take Miss Mattlock and get out of the country. It might be the only chance you have."

Spence grinned. "Perhaps you should be the one thinking about leaving. I have a perfect record in court, Umbridge. If I find one shred of proof, you're liable to end up behind bars."

"Did you ride all this way to threaten me?"

"No. I want to have a look at the sale record and deed for the Mattlock ranch."

"They're in order and perfectly legal, Kane. You won't have such an easy time of your case. Alvin Peek was given total control of the ranch after Miss Mattlock became crazy. He signed the deed over to me, and there isn't a thing that you can do about that."

"I'd still like to examine the papers. If necessary, I can always have the judge write out an order to force you to turn the documents over to me."

"That won't be necessary, Kane," Daton

said easily. "I have nothing to hide."

"Fine," Spence said, looking over Daton's shoulder at the approach of a young horseman. The rider was built like Daton, with the same fair hair and skin.

"My son, Aaron," Daton said. "I'll get those documents for you."

Spence didn't reply. He was still looking at Aaron, who seemed to be in his early twenties.

"You're Kane," Aaron said matter-of-factly, stopping his horse.

"That's right."

"I saw you take Strummer the other day. You're a good man with your fists."

"I've had a little practice," Spence admitted.

"Never seen a man who could jab with his left like you do. You crossed up Strummer with that. He's a bear in a fight."

"So I gathered."

There was no hostility in the young man's face. He just seemed mildly curious about Spence.

"What's your business here?"

"I'm representing Miss Mattlock. She's to have a new competency hearing in two weeks. Then she'll be wanting to get something back out of her place."

Aaron sighed. "I never did hold with sending her to that place, but there ain't nothing can be done about her ranch. Alvin sold it and lit out. He was a real weasel."

"What about your mother?" Spence asked carefully, watching for the young man's reaction.

"She was acting real strange. Sometimes she didn't know where she was or who any of us were. Did a lot of sleeping, too."

"Anyone been out here from town today?"

"Just you."

"Gloria Umbridge died last night," Spence told him solemnly.

Pain sprang into the young man's eyes. He seemed to swallow hard, looking down at the ground.

"How come no one from the ranch ever went to see her?" Spence asked.

"Pa thought it was best."

"What about him and Laura Woods?"

Aaron glared at Spence. "What do you mean by that?"

"Some talk around town says that your mother was the unwanted third party of a love triangle."

"I told you how it was!" Aaron snapped. "Ma didn't know us boys! She was in a stupor most of the time, kind of a daze. Doc Vanbough said he might be able to help her!"

"You believed that, knowing the record of the asylum?"

Suspicion filled the young man's eyes. "I know what you're trying to do, lawyer, but it won't work. I'm not going against my pa!"

"Tough man, your father," Spence said. "He gets what he wants. Just like having Cassie Mattlock put away, then buying her place. He's a man who controls his own destiny and the destiny of many around him. Like your mother. And then there's Laura Woods."

"He didn't begin seeing Miss Woods until Ma was taken to the asylum. He was lonely after that. He needed someone to talk to."

"What ever happened to the coal mine that Jerrod Steel owned?" Spence asked, changing the subject a bit.

"It had a mortgage against it," Aaron replied. "Pa always had the option to buy, so he picked up the deed. Sonny is over there running it now."

"Looks like you Umbridges might one day own the whole valley and Junction City."

Aaron laughed. "We already own everything we want in the valley, Kane. You go stirring up trouble against us, you'll find yourself facing every man in the country." He narrowed his eyes. "And all of them won't be satisfied to take you on with their fists."

"I'm a peace-loving man, Aaron. All I want is a little justice for my client."

"You'd better track down her stepbrother then. He's the one who took the money and ran out on her."

Daton came out to the porch. He held two pieces of paper in his hand. It seemed that his eyes flicked to his son and then to Spence with the light of suspicion, but it could have been the afternoon sun.

"Here you are, Lawyer Kane. You'll note that the bill of sale is marked 'paid in full' there at the bottom of the page."

Spence looked over the pages shortly, then handed them back. "I'd have said that the Mattlock place was worth three times what you paid, not counting the cattle."

Daton lifted a careless shoulder. "That isn't your concern, Kane. Alvin asked me what I would pay him and I told him. It's that simple."

"Hardly simple, but it does appear to have been legal ... unless I can prove you were an accomplice to setting Miss Mattlock up."

"Setting her up?"

"With the use of drugs," Spence said pointedly. "Your doctor friend has access to a number of potions that could make a person wander around in a stupor or seem dazed and uncertain. I'm for thinking you hired him to see that Miss Mattlock seemed just that way."

Daton laughed at the accusation, but Aaron put inquisitive eyes on his father.

"You are throwing stones wildly to see if you can hit anyone, Kane. I don't know what you're talking about."

"Your wife died last night, Daton," Spence said. "It appeared to me that she died for lack of treatment."

Daton didn't blink over the news of Gloria's death. He did look a bit closer at Spence, a dark shadow spreading over his face.

"I was told that Gloria had pneumonia. That's often fatal—regardless of the care."

"She'd been badly treated in that house of horrors, Daton. Probably chained and whipped. Did you also know about that?"

Aaron's head snapped around at that. He opened his mouth but was silenced by Daton's harsh reply.

"I'm not totally aware of everything that goes on at the asylum. And I know that you are very likely making up stories just to try and get a rise out of me. Well, you've seen your papers, and you've relayed the news of my wife's death. Now get off my ranch!"

Spence sighed. "Good day to you, Daton. I

hope you can sleep nights. I'd hate to see you go crazy and end up at that place yourself."

Then he rode out of the yard, leaving a strained silence between Aaron and his father.

CHAPTER ELEVEN

Instead of returning to town, Spence picked up the trail to the old Mattlock spread. He had a good excuse for going there, since Cassie probably still had some belongings somewhere on the ranch.

The Mattlock spread wasn't much at first glance, not when compared to Daton's huge place five miles away. The house was a mixture of sod and timber, with a sagging roof and run-down porch. But the land was good and had a river in the middle of it. When you added the Mattlock property to the Umbridge holdings, you really had something.

The yard was full of weeds, Spence saw, and the corral was broken in several places.

Only the barn had any sign of livestock. A single horse stood within the shadows. It was still saddled, patiently awaiting the return of its rider.

"Light down, Kane," a voice called from the interior of the house.

Spence couldn't see who had spoken but calmly reined his horse next to the hitching post in front of the house. He dismounted and tied the reins loosely. When he again looked up, a man was standing in the doorway.

"Kind of figured you'd be riding out this way," the man said easily.

"Miss Mattlock needs some of her things. I just dropped by to see if her clothes and belongings were still here."

The man wore two guns, a matching pearl-handled set with shiny conchos on black, glistening holsters. His boots were expensive, embroidered and adorned by Mexican spurs. He wore a leather vest and felt stetson hat. He wasn't as tall as Spence, nor was he heavy in build. But this was a man to watch out for. This was a man of danger.

"That isn't much of an excuse to come snooping," he said, appraising Spence with calculating eyes.

"It's the best I could do."

The man grinned. "My name is Sarton Joy,

but everyone calls me Sparks." His grin grew wider. "I guess I earned that name because of the way things seem to happen whenever I'm around. Make enough sparks fly, and someone is going to tag you with a suitable name."

"You seem to know my name already, Sparks. Why the interest?"

"The boss thinks someone ought to keep an eye on you. After what you did to Strummer, he figured that you might also be good with a gun."

"I'm afraid not. They don't do much shooting back in my hometown. We're more ... civilized than that."

"A civilized man can die real easy out here," Sparks warned. "You might do well to head on back home."

"Just as soon as I finish what I came for."

"What exactly did you come for, Kane?"

"The asylum needs cleaning up. It might need closing down. I'm authorized to investigate the place and report to the authorities."

"And that includes sticking your nose into the Mattlock affair?"

"You don't really believe that Cassandra Mattlock is crazy, do you?"

"I believe whatever my boss tells me to believe, Kane. If you're tying your brand to a herd, you ought to make certain that you latch onto the biggest bull of the lot."

"Do you mind if I take a look for Miss Mattlock's things?"

"Just don't be here fifteen minutes from now. I've got to ride up to see a couple of the boys. When I return, I want you gone from here. Understand?"

"You are threatening me?"

The man smiled. "I don't think that's necessary. Just be gone by the time I return."

"I'll do my best," Spence said.

"Good," Sparks said with another easy grin. "I'll be seeing you, lawyer. Let's hope that you keep your nose clean. Because you don't stand much of a chance against me."

"Strummer might have thought the same thing," Spence pointed out.

"That's right. But Strummer took you on with his fists. I'd be coming at you with guns, Kane. When I settle something, it'll be permanent."

"I'll remember."

Then Sparks Joy was crossing the yard to get his horse. He grinned once more, riding past Spence. There was something about his smile that sent a chill up a man's spine. Sparks was a killer—it shone in his eyes.

Aaron glared at his father. "I want it straight, Pa," he demanded. "Did you commit

Ma just so you could run after that woman in town?"

"Don't be a fool," Daton snarled. "You saw what that fancy-talking lawyer was up to. He wants to turn us against each other."

"I was here more than Sonny," Aaron said. "I watched Ma stagger about as if she was in a daze. Kane said that Vanbough had medicine to make people act that way. Did you drug her? Did you have her stuck into that awful place when there was nothing wrong with her?"

"I did what I thought was best for your mother," Daton insisted. "She became crazy. She never knew where she was, who we were, what was going on in the world. That lawyer was spouting off just to turn you against me. Don't be thinking I'd do that to your mother. I was married to her for twenty-six years, Aaron. You can't believe I'd do something like that."

But Aaron only shook his head. "I'm going to speak to Vanbough about it, Pa. If you sent our ma to that stinking pit to get rid of her, I'll forget that you're my father. I'll come back here and kill you."

"Aaron!" Daton cried. "Can you hear yourself? Do you realize you're doing just what Kane wants you to?"

"I'm going to find out if he was telling the

truth," Aaron said. "If he was lying, I'll be going after him."

"Don't be a fool, son!"

But Aaron was already turning toward the corral. His mother had always been a quiet woman, patiently putting up with her husband's terrible temper. Aaron had often felt that he hardly knew her, but he had loved her. And she had died alone in that rotten asylum, condemned to misery from the moment she'd set foot in the place. Aaron had known it, but he'd thought she was crazy. If not...

With the burning desire to learn the truth, he saddled his horse and rode out of the yard.

Spence checked the bundle of clothes and personal articles that were tied to the back of his saddle. These were the only things of Cassie's that he'd found at the ranch. They weren't much, but they were better than nothing.

As he rode to Junction City, he couldn't stop thinking of the girl, of her sad face, her soft blond hair. Then he wondered what it would be like to be married to her, married to Cassie Mattlock.

CHAPTER TWELVE

Emma Baily fixed two extra plates of food for the evening meal. Spence took them up to the attic, joining Cassie for supper. She seemed like a different person now that she was away from the asylum. And she was thrilled with the few possessions he'd found at her onetime home.

The girl ate with gusto, then apologized at the way she'd devoured the meal.

"It's quite understandable," Spence told her gently. "I imagine you ate little—and very bad—food in that house of horrors."

"That's true," she sighed. "And one of the men there is so hungry that he actually eats anything he finds on the floor—dead or alive. That place is worse than any jail I'd ever imagined."

"We'll try to change everything there later. First off, we need to prove you don't belong in the asylum."

"Will that be hard?"

"I'll have to wire for an out-of-town doctor to examine you. We'll need someone with credentials to go up against Vanbough."

"He can be very persuasive. He made me seem totally insane a couple of times."

"Tell me about it."

"Well, I don't remember a lot of what went on. I was in a fog after the death of Jerrod and my father. I remember sleeping much more than usual, and I couldn't think straight. Alvin had to do most of the cooking. I couldn't even manage that."

"Sounds as if you were drugged."

"I think so," she agreed. "I remember Vanbough coming out just after the funeral. He and Alvin spent some time together, but I didn't give it any thought. Then when I found out that they were calling me unbalanced and crazy, I tried to run away. I was so groggy that I fell off my horse. That was enough that I was put into Vanbough's custody until the hearing."

"What do you remember from that time?"

"It's strange, but I don't remember much at

all. I was sleeping most of the day, frightened at nights, and constantly forced to drink something bitter. Then the day before the hearing, I only got a drink of water and a little bread. I don't know what happened to me, but I was so...so weak and nervous the next morning that I acted sort of strange. During the hearing, I think I screamed at the judge and tried to run out. Everything is pretty hazy, but I remember being hysterical. I've never in my life been hysterical—except for that one single morning."

"Whatever potion or medicine they were giving you, they must have stopped it that last day. Your body was so used to it, though, that you became nervous and irrational."

"That sounds like the theory I came up with. I was so shaky that I couldn't even answer Vanbough's questions. It made me look as if I was crazy."

Spence put down his plate on a tiny table, as he'd finished eating. They were both sitting on a cot, for there was very little furniture in the small attic.

"What about your ranch?" he asked, changing the subject. "How much do you think the place is worth?"

"I could only guess. We had a small loan at the bank, and Pa would never speak of selling it."

"Does three thousand dollars sound fair?"

She frowned. "I'm not sure what we owed the bank, but the place had five hundred head of cattle. I shouldn't think that three thousand dollars would even pay for the herd."

"Alvin sold everything for that amount. I'll check with the banker tomorrow and see what the outstanding balance was on your place."

"What will any of that prove?" Cassie asked.

"Maybe nothing."

"Any word on where Alvin went?"

"No one seems to have any idea. Did he have any other relatives or friends that you know of?"

"Not that I know of. He'd mentioned going to California a couple of times, but I never thought he was serious."

"Well, it's a big country. If he changed his name, we'll probably never find him."

"Then I'm completely broke?"

"Unless your father had money in the bank or something stashed away that only you know about."

"No. We never had much extra money. The ranch always ate up the money with one thing and another."

Spence sighed. "Then we'll concentrate on gaining your freedom. It might be the only thing you get out of all this."

"Believe me," she said, "freedom is worth much more than any kind of wealth."

"Sort through your things, Miss Mattlock. Let me know if there's anything you need. All right?"

The girl's gray eyes glowed in the dim light from the lamp that lit the attic. She gazed intently at Spence, seeming to look for something.

"You've been a godsend, Mr. Kane. I'll never be able to repay you for what you've done for me."

"I was glad to do it," he assured her. "And I'm going to help all those other people, too."

With her hands folded in her lap, the girl looked very demure, rather shy but alluring. She tipped her head to one side, her lovely blond hair caressing one cheek.

"We will win the competency hearing, won't we?"

"I've got an unbroken record in court, ma'am," Spence told her with as much confidence as he could muster.

"Your wife must be very proud of you," she said.

"I have no wife," he replied. "In fact, other

than Nell Bethea, you're the only woman who's meant anything to me in the last few years."

"Nell Bethea?"

"I'll tell you about her sometime. She's quite a woman. But why don't you go to bed now? I'll stick around the place a lot to make sure no one comes looking for you. And I'm staying at the hotel just down the block. I shouldn't think anyone would look for you, but there might be more at stake here than just a hearing about your sanity."

"You mean the ranch?" Cassie asked.

"Mostly."

"But Daton has the ranch. Why should he care what happens to me now?"

"I just have a bad feeling about Daton. A man as ruthless and powerful as he could cause a lot more trouble. If he decides that he doesn't want me snooping around, and he doesn't want you asking questions about your stepbrother and the ranch, he might decide to kill both of us."

"Kill us?" She was incredulous.

"He had you committed. As far as he was concerned, you would have died in that asylum. That isn't exactly murder, but it isn't far from it either."

"You frighten me, Mr. Kane," she murmured.

"Don't get upset. We don't know what Daton will do just yet. If anything. I was only thinking out loud about an extreme possibility. I want you to stay hidden up here until the hearing. I know that it's confining, but I think it's safe."

"I'll do whatever you ask," she replied.

"Good," Spence said.

"But only on one condition."

He cocked an eyebrow. "Condition?"

"That you don't take any unnecessary risks. I couldn't live if I thought that I'd brought harm to you."

"We'll both play it safe," Spence said.

Then he picked up the dishes, walked over to the ladder, and gave the girl a reassuring smile.

"Things will work out fine, Miss Mattlock. You'll see."

A tight smile found its way to her lips. "I'll hold you to that, Mr. Kane."

He climbed down the ladder to the main floor of the Baily house. Cassie depended on him. He practically had her life in his hands. How would he live with himself if he failed her? He had to succeed!

Vanbough folded his arms across his chest as if bored with the conversation. Aaron Umbridge had confronted him, asking him questions about his mother, but the doctor was very cool, very controlled.

"Did you drug Cassie Mattlock?" Aaron suddenly said.

"What does Cassie have to do with your mother?"

"I want to know."

"What did your father tell you?" Dr. Vanbough asked.

"Nothing. But—"

"Then I have nothing to tell you either. You yourself saw how Cassie acted at the hearing. Had you ever heard her scream and rant before?"

"No," Aaron said.

"And your mother, wasn't she acting very strange before she was committed? Didn't she have trouble even recognizing you and your brother?"

"Yes, but—"

"Then I don't see what you want from me, Aaron. I told your father that your mother had pneumonia. She received the best treatment possible, but she was simply too sick to survive. She died in her sleep, quite painlessly."

"What about the story I heard about her being chained and whipped?"

"I don't know where you get your information. Your mother was docile and very easy to manage. She required no restraint or physical discipline. This is not a house of torture, Aaron. We treat crazy people here...as humanely as possible."

"Then you swear she was never chained?"

"As I just said, your mother didn't require any restraint at all. She was quite willing to do what we told her."

"And Cassie?"

"What does the Mattlock girl have to do with your mother?"

"I'm the curious type," Aaron said.

"Cassie was punished once for fighting with another inmate. I don't think that she started it, but we often punish both parties when there's a dispute. That helps to control the populace. If she was ever chained, I'm not aware of it. But it wouldn't have happened without a reason."

Aaron stepped closer to the doctor. "Tell me the truth, Vanbough. Did my mother really have to come to this place?"

"She was in need of treatment, Aaron. I don't know how she would have fared at home. She wasn't dangerous, but she would have gotten worse and worse every day."

"Did she ever talk about any of us?"

"Gloria never said a word during her time with us. She was very withdrawn. I don't know that she would have ever recovered, for

I could hardly get her to pay attention to me. If the patient refuses treatment, there's no way to help them."

"Did you give her any drugs?"

"Some to help her sleep. Why?"

"Her symptoms were very much the same as Cassie's, don't you agree?"

"I suppose," the doctor said.

"And both sets of symptoms could have been caused by drugs. Isn't that right?"

"I don't know what you're getting at, Aaron. There are some drugs that might affect the way a person acts, but the effects wouldn't go on and on."

"Unless the person keeps getting the drug again and again."

"Are you accusing me of something?"

Aaron wanted to grab the man, to shake the truth out of him. But what if he was telling the truth? What if his mother had been slowly going mad, crawling into a shell? After all, she had always been a withdrawn, very quiet sort of person. It was possible that there had been no foul play at all.

"I'll be seeing you, Vanbough," he told the doctor.

"Come and visit anytime at all."

Then Aaron was out in the evening air. He had to do some thinking. Maybe a drink would help. There were too many angles, too many possibilities, clouding his mind. If he could clear his head, maybe he'd sort out the important details.

CHAPTER THIRTEEN

Spence heard something outside his hotel room and suddenly sat upright in his bed. He reached instinctively for the gun he'd placed on the nightstand.

"Who is it?"

"Me," a very small voice said through the door. "I have to talk to you."

Fumbling to turn up the lamp, Spence hurried over to open the door. A barefoot Cassie scooted through at once, a shawl over her head and shoulders.

"What on earth is it, Miss Mattlock?"

She put a finger to her lips to hush him. He stuck his head out the door and saw a man coming down the hall. Spence calmly closed the door. The man kept walking to a room farther down the hall.

"It's all right," Spence assured the girl. "That man is staying here at the hotel. He's some sort of drummer."

Cassie removed her shawl, placing it over the rail at the foot of the bed. She was out of breath, evidently from running to the hotel from the Baily house.

"What are you doing here? And why don't you even have your shoes on?"

"I didn't think about shoes," she admitted meekly. "I—when I discovered this with the things you brought me..." She pulled out a small flint arrowhead and thin chain from her pocket. "Where did you get it?"

"From your ranch. It was on the floor among some of the trash that had been strewn around. It was together with some of your other things. It didn't look valuable, but I thought that it might be a keepsake of some kind."

"It was," she said firmly. "But not mine. My stepbrother was crazy about it. As a boy, it was the dearest possession he owned."

Spence frowned. "Maybe he outgrew the attachment."

"No. He often wore it for good luck. He wouldn't have left it behind...not in a hundred years!"

Spence waited until Cassie had seated herself on the edge of his bed. Then he moved over to sit down next to her.

"You know what you're implying, don't you?"

"Alvin wouldn't have left without his good-luck piece, Mr. Kane. I'm sure of it."

"Where was your father buried?" Spence asked.

"At the family cemetery, behind the house."

"And Jerrod?"

She looked a bit perplexed by his line of questioning. "Here in town. Why?"

"How many graves behind your house?"

"Ma, Pa, my stepma, Grandma, and an uncle."

"There were six graves there today, Miss Mattlock. You're quite certain of the number?"

She swallowed. "Grandpa was killed during the Ute war. There was no marker put up for him in the family cemetery. There should be five graves!"

"Perhaps Alvin didn't sell you out after all, then."

Cassie's eyes were wide, her mouth open, but she couldn't speak.

"I think that Alvin is that sixth grave, Miss Mattlock. If you give me permission, I'll look into it."

"B-but the place isn't mine."

"You are my client. If this case turns into murder, I won't just be defending you, I'll be representing you. We need to know who's in that grave. If it is Alvin, you'll be in great danger."

"Me?" she said. "It's you, Mr. Kane. You would be the target. They could always throw me back into that foul rat-infested prison. But you would have to be killed! Look, why don't you get away now, tonight? It isn't right to risk your life over this."

"What about you?" he said.

"I'll go someplace else. I'll make a new life for myself away from Junction City."

Spence felt a deep anger burn within him. "The law is no good until it stands for justice, Miss Mattlock. I haven't been a very good lawyer up to now because I couldn't really defend men who were guilty. If I'd have tried harder, I might have gotten some of them off, but they were all guilty as sin! Now you're innocent. And I just have to help you. To walk away from this—a possible murder, the fact that they threw you into that madhouse —I can't do it!"

"I hate to be cowardly, Mr. Kane," Cassie murmured softly. "But I can't stand the thought of returning to that asylum. I know you're right, that you have the proper outlook about law and justice, but...but...I'm so afraid. Oh, why don't we both just go away from here?"

Spence took the girl into his arms, holding her close. She didn't resist, slipping her own arms around his waist. She put her head against his chest, too.

"We have to also consider the others, Cassie," Spence said gently. "There are people like Gloria, who are dumped into the Country Acre Asylum to get them out of the way, helpless children like Jenny. How can we walk away from them?"

"Poor little Jenny," Cassie sighed. "If she only had someone to love her. She'll never be normal—not like other children her age—but she would be a joy to have around. She has so much love to give, so much life to share. It isn't fair that she's condemned to stay at such a horrible place."

"I intend to rectify that situation. I want to make things better for all those people. If I can do something like that, really help people, it would make Nell proud of me."

"You mentioned her before," Cassie said. "Who is she?"

"She's quite a woman. I don't think I'd have ever managed law school without her to lean on."

"You think a great deal of her...don't you?" Cassie's voice was strangely quiet.

"A perfect lady. She'll never get the amount of credit due her, but she's the most valuable woman I've ever known."

"Is she pretty?"

He cocked an eyebrow at her. "Pretty?"

"Well, you've been talking what a wonderful person she is, and you have a deep respect in your voice just mentioning her name. I was just wondering..."

"Yes, I'd say that Nell Bethea is a beautiful person, Cassie. She's a giving, compassionate woman, dedicated to the success of young men. There can't be any greater beauty than working to help others."

"I wasn't..." Cassie seemed to struggle with what she wanted to say. "I didn't mean to pry. I only wanted to know how you felt about her."

"I suppose I love her," he replied seriously. At the sudden way the girl lowered her gaze, he had to smile. "In fact, I love her as much as if she were my own mother."

Cassie's head popped back up. *"Mother?"*

"Nell is a lovely middle-aged woman. I stayed at her boardinghouse while I was going to law school."

"Then you and she—I mean, you're not..."

He smiled and gently kissed her.

* * *

Aaron stared into the glass of whiskey. He wasn't a drinking man. He hated the foul taste of liquor. He hated the foggy feeling a man had the next day. But tonight he'd thought a drink or two might help him.

"Hey, Aaron!" a familiar voice suddenly said.

Aaron turned to the man next to him at the bar. It was Sonny, his younger brother by fifteen months.

"Howdy, Sonny. Where you been keeping yourself?"

"That coal mine is work. We loaded up twelve wagons today. I think there might be a future in that stuff."

"Who's buying so much coal?" Aaron asked.

"You name it. Lotsa folks. Jerrod knew what he was doing. He's got several contracts with big business outfits. Add to that all the small outfits that burn coal instead of wood, and we've got a thriving business."

Aaron changed the subject. "You hear about Ma?"

Sonny sobered at once. "The judge rode by today and gave me the bad news." He sighed deeply. "I was hoping that she might get better."

"Kane—that man from Denver—says that

she was drugged to get rid of her. He thinks Pa was after Laura Woods."

Sonny bridled. "I've heard Kane has a big mouth. If I had time, I'd show him how to keep it closed!"

"He took Strummer," Aaron said. "I saw him do it."

"I heard. Must have been quite a fight."

"Not really. Kane was never in trouble."

Sonny asked, "He's that good?"

"I wouldn't bet against him—no matter who he fought."

Sonny let out a soft whistle. "He must be good."

"I spoke to Vanbough about Ma. I said that she and Cassie Mattlock had a lot of similar symptoms. Might have been more than just a coincidence."

That clouded Sonny's face once more. "Pa wouldn't do that—not to Ma!"

Aaron shrugged. "You know how he took after the Woods woman. Once she came to town, he was always finding an excuse to ride in for something."

"You—really think he just wanted to get rid of Ma?"

"I don't know, Sonny. I talked to Vanbough, but he didn't admit anything. All I'm going on is hunches and a few things Kane said. I don't like that man, but he got Cassie out and is demanding a new hearing. If there's nothing wrong with her, then how do we know something was really wrong with our mother?"

"This sounds serious, Aaron. What if we find out that our old man put Ma into the asylum just to get rid of her?"

"You remember that both Pa and Vanbough warned against us going to see her. What if that was to keep us from finding out she wasn't crazy at all?"

"But how'll we ever find out now?"

"I mean to talk to Cassie. She was in there with Ma," Aaron said.

"Think she'll talk to you?" Sonny asked.

"Why shouldn't she?"

"We own her farm now," Sonny pointed out. "Besides which, I'm working the mine that her fella owned. She might feel a little put out about that."

"Alvin sold her out, not you or me," Aaron said.

"Yes, but..." Sonny's voice trailed away.

"But what?" Aaron demanded.

"There are a couple things I know that you don't, big brother."

"Such as?"

"Who killed Joe Mattlock and Jerrod Steel."

Aaron said, "Rustlers killed them."

Sonny shook his head negatively. "It was Sparks and Monnahan. I heard them talking outside the mine a few weeks back. Mutt Monnahan was sore because he was stuck in the mine digging out coal. Sparks told him it was for his own good because he had a habit of drinking and doing too much talking."

"Why would..." But Aaron stopped in mid-sentence. He knew that Sparks only acted on his father's orders. The death of Joe Mattlock had been ordered.

Aaron went on. "Then there's no doubt that Vanbough drugged Cassie. It left only that sucker, Alvin, to deal with over the ranch."

"I was surprised that Pa offered him three thousand dollars. After buying up the mortgage on the coal mine, I thought we were pretty near broke until roundup."

Aaron tipped the glass of rotgut to his lips, almost gagging at the awful taste. "I'm going to talk to Cassie."

"How can you? We don't even know where she's at."

"That fancy lawyer will know. I'll go ask him right now."

"And if he won't tell us?"

Aaron tapped his holster. "I aim to find out, one way or the other!"

CHAPTER FOURTEEN

Spence was more than a little surprised to find Aaron and another young man at his door. He quickly rushed over to block the doorway.

"A little late for social calls, isn't it, Aaron?"

"I'm looking for Cassandra Mattlock," Aaron replied. "Me and Sonny would like to ask her a couple questions about our ma."

"Well, I don't know if—"

"It's all right," Cassie said, coming into Aaron and Sonny's view. "I'll tell them whatever I can."

Spence stepped back, allowing the two men to enter. Then he closed the door behind them. It was obvious that they hadn't expected to find the girl in his room.

"We were talking about the upcoming hearing," Spence told the two Umbridge boys. "I guess we can set aside our talk for the time being."

Aaron removed his hat. After elbowing Sonny, prompting him to do the same, the two of them stood before Cassie.

"Kane thinks that you were drugged," Aaron said. "He claims you were always sane, that the doctor from the asylum made you look crazy."

"I suffered a lot of grief at the loss of my father, but it didn't destroy my mind," she answered. "Vanbough and Alvin plotted to put me away. It left Alvin free to sell the ranch."

"We're right sorry for that," Aaron said sincerely. "Pa and Alvin worked on that scheme alone. Sonny was busy at the mine, and I kind of ramrod the ranch. We didn't have anything to do with that."

"You couldn't have gone against your father, even had you known," she said.

"About our mother," Sonny said quietly. "How'd she seem to act at the home? I mean, did she know where she was, what had happened to her?"

"Gloria didn't talk much to anyone. She stayed by herself, never caused any trouble, and hardly said a word to me. As for being mad or crazy, though, I don't believe that for a moment."

Sonny lowered his head. Aaron turned the hat in his hands. He couldn't meet Cassie's eyes.

"Did she . . . suffer much?" Aaron asked.

"More than she deserved," Cassie said. "She was only chained once, but she was treated like the rest of us—with contempt!"

"We didn't know," Sonny said lamely.

"You should have known!" Cassie fumed. "You should have cared enough to know!"

Aaron said, "Pa told us the doctor didn't want us troubling her. He said that total separation was needed. Well, aren't we supposed to take the word of our own father?"

"I don't have to live with your conscience, Aaron," she answered. "All I know is that your mother was shoved into that dirty, sleazy hole, forced to sleep with lice and bedbugs, given food that most dogs wouldn't eat. She was treated worse than most animals, and only because your father wanted to be rid of her. I know just how bad it was. I was right there at her side."

Cassie glared at the two brothers a moment. "I've taken three baths since I got away from there," she went on. "I've washed my hair until my scalp hurts. The filth alone is more than a normal person can bear. The death of your mother is proof of that!"

Aaron nudged Sonny. The two of them turned for the door. "Thanks for your time, Miss Mattlock," Aaron said. "We had to know."

"What will you do about it?" Spence asked the two boys.

Aaron looked at him but only shook his head. Then the pair were gone from the room. As Spence closed the door, Cassie came up to him.

"I was a little hard on them, wasn't I?"

"Not as hard as it must have been on Gloria. It's likely that she died of a broken heart as much as the pneumonia."

"I wonder what they'll do about it," Cassie said.

"After meeting Daton, I don't see them doing much of anything."

"I should have asked them about Alvin."

"I don't think they know anything about Alvin. In fact, I'm betting the boys are pretty ignorant about all that Daton is mixed up with."

"He does have some real shady characters on his payroll."

"I met Sparks Joy. He warned me not to get too inquisitive."

"Sparks has killed men before," Cassie said.

"I can believe that. This won't be an easy business."

"Have you thought up a plan of action?" she asked.

Spence grinned. "I thought I might mention the fact that I could be killed. It might get me another good-night kiss."

Cassie's face brightened, but she kept her distance. "I think you'd better take me home. My father warned me about men who would try and play on my sympathies."

"Fathers are the biggest handicap young men have when it comes to courting a lady."

"When your time comes, you'll be no different," she teased. "You'll be just as protective of your daughter as any other father."

"I imagine you're right about that."

Sparks stood in the dark alley, watching the two Umbridge boys come out of the hotel, wondering who they'd been talking to. He'd barely arrived in town in time to see Sonny go into the saloon to join Aaron. The two had been engrossed in their conversation, looking very somber. Somber and sad. Sparks had never seen them so serious before. Then they'd left the saloon and entered the hotel.

Sparks had watched and waited. Finally the pair left the hotel.

Sparks was about to leave his hiding place when he saw two more people leave the hotel: Spencer Kane and Cassie Mattlock.

The lawyer swept the area with his eyes, looking almost directly at Sparks Joy. Then he escorted the slender Cassie to the Baily store.

"So that's where you hid the girl," Sparks muttered smugly to himself.

He grinned at that, for it might help to know where Cassie was holed up. If trouble came, she might be the lever they would need to pry the snoopy lawyer away from the valley. Daton was afraid of having the girl running loose. He thought that she would spill the news of how Gloria shouldn't have been sent to the asylum.

Sparks Joy moved silently in the darkness, getting into a position to see the back of Baily's place. The lawyer opened the door for Cassie, but she didn't go right in. Instead, she leaned over and kissed him!

"Well, well," Sparks said. "It looks as if Cassie has found more than just a fancy lawyer to plead her case."

Kane said a few words to the girl that didn't reach Sparks's ears. Then the two of them parted. The lawyer looked around once more, but Sparks remained deep in the shadows. His fingers laced the butt of the heavy gun on his right hip. He should kill the man—kill him at once. Kane was going to be nothing but trouble.

Still, Sparks did not draw his gun. He had his orders. He was only to observe, to see what was going on in town.

There could be little doubt that the Umbridge boys had gone to visit Cassie and the lawyer. Maybe that might change Daton's outlook. Maybe he would agree that Kane had to be killed—before he found out that Alvin had never left the valley. Kane could cause too much trouble for a lot of people.

Moving stealthily, Sparks hurried through the streets of the town. He reached his horse and rode into the night. Daton would have to listen to him now. Spencer Kane was too dangerous to live. If Sonny and Aaron turned against Daton, he would blame Sparks for not getting rid of Kane right off.

Sparks dug his heels into his horse. The sooner he acted, the better. But he needed approval from Daton first. Once he had the go-ahead, he would rid the country of Spencer Kane.

CHAPTER FIFTEEN

Spence stood with his arms folded, steadfast, unmovable. "I want that order, Judge. There are only supposed to be five graves on the Mattlock spread. There is a sixth that must have a body in it. I intend to find out whose body that is!"

"But it's on Daton Umbridge's land now. Perhaps one of his men was killed in some sort of accident. He could have buried the man there."

"I don't want supposition, Judge Clott. I want positive proof!"

The judge paced the room, rubbing his hands together. "You are trying to upset the entire valley, Kane. Why stick your nose into something like this? I'll look more kindly on your plea for Miss Mattlock if you quit making such a confounded nuisance of yourself!"

"I assure you, Judge, I have the authority to get you taken off the bench. Either you comply with my demand, or I'll be forced to wire Governor Routt." Would his bluff work?

"All right! All right!" the judge exclaimed, throwing his hands up into the air. "But don't blame me if you get someone killed over this."

"You're supposed to represent justice in this land, Clott. I don't think you take your job seriously."

The man glowered at Spence. "You don't know what you're up against out here, Kane. You can't sit in judgment on everything and expect to live very long. You have to make allowances for the primitive conditions out here. There is only the law of the people here. If I go against the most powerful men, I'll have no authority at all. Isn't it better to have order and peace, rather than bloodshed and killing?"

"It depends on the price, Judge. If only one innocent person is killed or sent to that asylum, it's too high a price to pay."

Clott shook his head. "I don't think you'd last very long over here, Kane. It would be best for all concerned to move up the date of

Miss Mattlock's hearing and get it over with. You could win the case right now, and you'd be free to return home to Denver. You stick that nose of yours into places it doesn't belong, you're going to get a bullet in your snoot!"

"I'll look after my own nose. Your responsibility is to serve the summons, warrants, or papers needed to bring a case to trial or a corpse to light."

"I know the requirements of my job, Kane," the man grunted. "What is it specifically that you need?"

Junction City had a town marshal, but he was not the outgoing sort. In fact, Riley O'Shay didn't investigate anything that took place out of the town. He'd been something of a Civil War hero, but few people in Colorado paid him any mind. With that war ten years past, Riley O'Shay was just a very minor piece of history, another Yankee who'd done his duty.

Spence reported his findings at the asylum and outlined what he had in mind. O'Shay gave him the courtesy of listening, but that was all.

"You're plumb crazy, son!" he laughed cynically. "You can't go digging up graves on Daton Umbridge's property."

"I have a court order here that—"

But Riley held up a hand to stop Spence's argument. "It don't matter what kind of paper you got, son. Ain't no one going to tread on Daton's turf. Thunderation, son, he pays my wages!"

"You wear a badge," Spence pointed out. "Doesn't that mean anything to you?"

"If you mean, why ain't I ready to buck Daton and get myself out of a job or maybe killed, forget it. I done my duty to my country once. I come away with a hole in my leg and a medal pinned to my chest. When it gets cold, that medal don't help the pain that sets into my old wound. I'm not risking my life for anyone else again."

Spence shook his head. "The war didn't teach you a blessed thing, Marshal. You're about as ignorant as any man I've met when it comes to fighting for human rights."

"I risked my life!" the older man cried. "I was a darn good soldier!"

"But you were never a real man, O'Shay. You don't do what you know is right without being ordered to do it. Well, I can't order you to ride out to the old Mattlock place with me. If you want to hide here behind the skirts of the town, not risking any of Daton's wrath, I can only pity the image you've given these people for all the years since the war. You've lost your nerve, O'Shay. It's that simple."

"Yeah?" he cried. "What would you know about putting your life on the line? Have you ever been caught in a bloody battle, with cannons blasting away, men dying all around you, with disease and frost, with heat and cold, with rain and mud all eating your body? You ain't got the right to talk to me like I was some fool, son. I earned my place in society."

"Too bad you didn't remain in it, Marshal," Spence told him dryly. "You don't belong behind a badge."

The marshal blurted something back, but Spence was already going out the door. He would get no help from O'Shay.

Spence had a horse saddled and readied at the livery. He was glad to get the same horse he'd been riding since he'd come to town. The mare was strong, durable, and had an easy canter. As he led the animal out of the barn, he saw Bob Baily coming up the street.

"Hold up, Kane," Baily called. "I'm going with you."

Spence waited, even helping to get Bob's horse saddled. As the man climbed aboard, Kane looked at him.

"This isn't a very smart move, Bob. Everyone will suspect that you asked for an investigation."

"Ain't that way at all, Kane," he grinned. "The marshal asked me to ride out with you. He said that someone would be needed to identify the body you uncover. It'll be tough, after two months or more, even recognizing any body."

"So O'Shay's conscience got the better of him, did it?"

"You must have ruffled his feathers pretty good. He didn't exactly ask me to come, he practically threatened me. I never have seen him so huffy."

"I kind of stepped on his pride."

"You been stepping on a few toes, Kane. I hope one of those people don't take serious offense and blow your brains out. Well, I see you brought a rifle with you. Hope we don't need it."

"It's a possibility that I've been worrying about," Spence said.

"Got a shovel?"

"There were some garden tools at the Mattlock place."

"Let's go then, Kane. I'm more than a little anxious to get this investigative work behind us."

Daton looked at his two sons, his anger barely controlled. They had never stood up against him before, never questioned him or his actions. This was all due to that meddling lawyer, Spencer Kane!

"We want to hear you say it, Pa," Aaron told him. "Tell us the truth straight out. Did you send our mother to the asylum to die?"

"The asylum is a place where they care for crazy people," he replied calmly, suppressing his rage. "There was no reason to believe that your mother would die there so soon of pneumonia."

Aaron said, "Vanbough was out here a couple of weeks before Ma started acting funny. I remember that she started drinking that special tea each morning. It was to help her hay fever attacks."

"That's all it was," Daton told them.

"I think that same drug that made Cassie look crazy was in that tea, Pa," Aaron said boldly. "I think our mother was drugged into that mindless stupor."

"Why would the doctor want her drugged?"

"Only one reason we can think of," Aaron continued. "You wanted to get rid of her."

"That's ridiculous!"

"It is?" Sonny asked. "You used to hit Ma and scream at her a lot. You gave her hell for nothing."

"You couldn't have really loved our mother," Aaron said. "I never saw you once kiss her, not in my whole life."

"She was a distant, cold person," Daton said. "I was tough on her because she expected it. She wouldn't have been worth two bits, if I hadn't have kept after her all the time."

"What we want to know, Daton," Aaron said, calling his father by his first name for the first time, "is this. Did you have a hand in drugging our ma?"

Daton raised his right hand. "I swear to you boys, I didn't have anything to do with making your mother look crazy. If Vanbough did put something in that tea, I can only think he did it for his own gain."

"What gain?" Sonny asked.

"He probably thought that I would give more money to his home. With Gloria in there, I did contribute more money. I wanted her taken care of properly."

"And what about Laura Woods?" Sonny said.

"Laura has been a good friend of mine. She and your mother were even friends. Why it's her that is dressing your ma for her funeral. There ain't nothing else between us."

Aaron and Sonny exchanged looks. They'd never seen their father in such a light. He'd never before stopped to explain anything to them. Whether he was feeling a sense of guilt, or if he simply was beginning to see them as men and not boys was the question.

"We've got a heap of work piling up, sons," Daton said. "Nothing we do now can bring back Gloria to us. We've got to go on with our work. You can be proud that she was your mother, for she was a fine, wonderful woman. I've ordered the biggest headstone for the grave that has ever been installed in the town cemetery. She's gone from us now, but she'll not be forgotten."

Aaron lowered his head in defeat. Daton could have been guilty of about anything, but he was still their father, still the powerful baron of the valley. As a family, they would rule their empire together.

"Let's go," Sonny prompted. "I've got several wagons to get loaded."

Aaron nodded. "I've kind of let work get out of hand as well. I'll go check on the herds today."

"That's fine, boys," Daton told them. "We'll keep things running smooth, just like nothing ever happened."

CHAPTER SIXTEEN

Bob didn't examine the body for more than a second. Then he covered the corpse's head with the dirty blanket it had been wrapped in. He looked up at Spence.

"Ain't much doubt now, Kane," he said hoarsely. "This is Alvin Peek. There's a bullet hole through the base of his neck."

"Then he didn't take the money from the ranch and ride off."

"You can bet there isn't any money buried with him."

Spence took hold of the dead man's legs, putting him back into his grave, with Bob handling the upper end. They covered him in silence. When they'd finished, they returned their tools to the small shed next to the house.

"It looks as if you've uncovered more than just a grave here, Kane. I'd say that—"

A blast from a gun stopped Bob's words. He was knocked over as the bullet hit him.

Spence ducked quickly into the shed, a second bullet chipping the doorframe. He pulled out his gun, relieved to see that Bob was crawling into the shed as well.

"You hit bad?"

"It ain't good," Bob grunted. "But you worry about that bushwhacker—not about me!"

Spence did just that. He spotted the gunman moving from behind the house. Spence opened fire at him, squeezing off two quick rounds. It sent the man scurrying back where he came from.

"I'm not much good with a handgun," Spence told Baily. "If I can get my rifle..."

The man's next shot chipped wood just above his head. He had to duck back into the shed.

"I fear that gunman doesn't suffer the same handicap as you, Kane," Baily observed. "He has us pinned in here."

The horses were tied twenty yards away, by the family cemetery. To get to them and the rifle, Spence would have to expose himself to gunfire. He decided to take the risk. The gunman shot at him once more—and barely missed. But Spence had the upper hand once he reached his rifle. It wasn't long before the gunman had been hit in the chest and fell facedown to the ground.

Spence kept his rifle on the fallen man as he walked toward him, but he knew he wouldn't be shooting anyone again. He turned the man over with his foot, sticking the rifle barrel right into the man's face.

"Who are you, and why did you try to kill us?"

The man's face was twisted with pain, his eyes glazed. He rolled his head back and forth, his mouth working, but no words came out.

Dropping to his knees, Spence knocked the revolver out of the man's hand. Then he looked at the bullet hole. He was not a doctor, but this gunman didn't have very long.

"Why'd you try and kill us?"

"S-Sparks...gonnna...get...get you!" the man grunted. "You...you won't..." But the threat died on his lips.

Spence left him where he'd fallen, returning to the shed. He found Baily sitting up, a hand placed tightly against a bloody shoulder. Bob let out a sigh of relief on seeing Spence return.

"I heard the shooting, but I didn't know who to expect back. I never figured a city slicker like you to have a chance against Mutt Monnahan."

"That's who that man was?"

"You say was. Did you kill him?"

"It wasn't a gun battle to be put into any history books, but, yes, I managed to kill him before he did me in. Then he threatened that Sparks Joy would kill me."

"Can't be much doubt about who's behind all of this, Kane. Mutt was trying to cover up for the killing of Alvin Peek."

"That might not prove a thing against Daton."

"But Mutt was on Daton's payroll!"

"He could have killed Alvin for the three thousand dollars his boss had paid the man. His shooting at us could be construed to show that he was acting on his own."

"You don't believe that, do you?"

Spence was making a temporary bandage as they talked. He soon had Bob's wound packed tightly, but he knew he needed to get the man back to town.

"What I believe isn't important, Bob, not in a court of law. We need evidence, hard facts. Mutt's trying to kill us doesn't implicate anyone in the eyes of the court."

"Then the court is blind!"

Spence put an arm under Baily and helped him to his feet. Then they were staggering toward the horses. Next Spence draped Mutt over his horse, which had been tethered nearby.

Sparks dropped the cigarette he'd been smoking, crushing it out with his heel. He had expected Mutt to come riding back into town, but that hadn't happened. Instead, Mutt was draped over the saddle of his horse. Spencer Kane led the animal, also helping to steady Bob Baily on his horse. A few people surged forward, two helping the wounded postmaster down. It provided enough confusion so that Sparks was able to slip down a side street unobserved and pick up his own horse.

Once away from town, he put his heels to his mount. Sparks was shocked that Mutt had failed. He couldn't believe Kane could take him in a gunfight, but the positive proof was there. Mutt had managed to wound Baily, but Kane had killed him. The man was full of surprises.

It was only a short ride to Daton's ranch. Sparks kept the horse at a lathered pace until he spotted Daton Umbridge. The rancher was eagerly awaiting word of Kane's death. He even rode over to meet Sparks—something he seldom did.

Sparks pulled up, stopping his horse, confronting his curious employer. Then he let out a long sigh.

"Mutt is dead."

"What?" Daton shouted. "But you said that—"

"I know," Sparks snapped. "I thought he could take that fancy jack lawyer. Who'd have ever thought Mutt couldn't handle Kane?"

"What happened?" Daton asked.

"I don't know for sure. Baily went with Kane to the Mattlock place. According to that paper Clott gave Kane, he had permission to dig up the graves in the family cemetery."

"That means they found Alvin," Daton said.

"It would seem so."

Daton let out a long breath. "Blast it! How does that man do it? He has drawn aces to every hand!"

"It might just be dumb luck," Sparks said.

"Did dumb luck kill Mutt Monnahan?" Daton growled.

"I should have backed his play. I was busy making sure that I had a good alibi in town, but maybe I should have risked being in on it. At least Kane would be dead now."

"Baily wasn't supposed to be in this pot. I don't want the town turning against us. Baily is popular."

"Just how do we stop Kane now?" Sparks asked.

Daton thought for a long moment. "Killing him now would only make things look worse for us. If Mutt had killed him out at the Mattlock place, it would have been simple. The man was trespassing. We didn't know about any paper the judge had given him. Mutt was at fault for killing him, and I'd have made a big deal out of getting after Mutt. We might have even worked a deal with Clott to make Mutt do a little time for the shooting. For the right wages, Mutt would have served a year or two in the pen."

"And now?"

"We'll have to do things different. We had our chance to do this out in the open, but we failed. It would seem that we'll have to work the plan in a more snaky way."

"What have you got in mind?"

Daton looked at Sparks, but his mind was elsewhere. "You said that Kane and the Mattlock girl appeared to be more than just a lawyer and client?"

"I seen him kiss her."

"Cassie wouldn't allow a man to kiss her unless there was something very special between them. I'm not sure that even Jerrod ever kissed the girl. I think Miss Mattlock is the key to our next action, Sparks. Here's what we'll do."

CHAPTER SEVENTEEN

Spence waited impatiently as the retired old doctor of Junction City, Jed Blaine, tended to Bob's wound in the next room. Leaving the sanctity of her small attic, Cassie was also present. By the time the old doctor finished, Judge Clott was in the doctor's sitting room as well.

"I saw Mutt Monnahan, Kane," he said through clenched teeth. "Just what good did it do me to write out that paper, giving you permission to dig up that grave? You managed to get someone killed over it all the same!"

"Mutt didn't ask to see any paper, Judge. He came in shooting, and the only way I could stop him was to shoot back."

The judge looked over at Cassie. "What about Alvin?"

Spence said, "It was his body in that extra grave. The money he supposedly received from the sale of the ranch wasn't buried with him. Mutt might have killed him for that money, then buried him in the cemetery."

"You've no proof of that," the judge said.

"No. It could just have easily been on Daton's orders, but there isn't any evidence of that either."

"Then you've gained nothing," Clott grunted, folding his arms. "You're like a coyote among a herd of cattle, Kane. You stir things up, excite everyone, but you have no idea what you aim to do with all of the cows. You're nothing but trouble."

"There should be an investigation into the murder of Alvin Peek. I also think the papers that were supposedly signed by him should be brought in as evidence. That signature might not even be his own."

"You're looking to start a real war, Kane," Clott grumbled. "I can't go hounding Daton Umbridge about the legality of his deed. That man pays most of my wages. His crew supports a good share of Junction City."

"That has nothing to do with the law and justice, Judge."

"It certainly has to do with common sense and survival, Kane. You start bucking Daton, you'll end up bucking the whole town. They need that man and his money to get by."

"So we look the other way, is that it?" Spence said.

"I didn't say that."

"You might as well have, Clott," Spence snapped. "Look at the facts! Joe Mattlock was killed, Jerrod Steel was killed, Gloria Umbridge was put away and died, Cassie Mattlock was put away, and now Alvin Peek is discovered to be dead! What more do you need to start some kind of investigation? How many people have to die or be committed before you think it's time to act?"

Clott threw up his hands. "I want nothing to do with it. I've done all that I'm going to do!"

"Then I'll have you investigated, Clott. I'll have you separated from that robe that makes you think that you have the right to sit in judgment of other men. When you cease to act justly, you no longer are qualified to be a judge."

The words bounced harmlessly off Clott. He was picking up his hat and turning for the door.

"You have a sworn duty, Clott!" Spence said.

The judge opened the door and looked over his shoulder at the lawyer.

"I have no obligation to forfeit my life,

Kane. Once you're dead and gone, I'll resume my control of the judiciary system in Junction City." He shook his head in distaste. "I don't think that I'll have long to wait."

Spence watched the man disappear out the door, then sighed heavily. He'd failed to prod the judge into aiding him. It made his job a whole lot tougher now, for he didn't have any local support.

"What will you do?" Cassie asked quietly.

Spence smiled at her. "The case is crystal clear, my dear Cassandra," he said lightly. "I shall force the conscience-ridden Daton into a confession. Then it will be but a small matter to close down the asylum until a team of real doctors and trained workers can arrive. If Colorado gains statehood next year, there'll be funds provided for proper institutions."

"It sounds so simple."

"There is hardly a catch to the plan," he said. "So long as Daton goes along with my scheme."

The doctor entered the room, coming out of the adjacent bedroom. He moved stiffly, bent with age.

"No trouble," he said. "Bob will make it all right."

"That's great!" Spence said.

"He'll need a few days' rest, however. He lost a lot of blood on the ride home."

"Thanks, Dr. Blaine," Spence added.

The old man looked over the rims of his half-moon glasses. He regarded Spence for a long moment.

"You've taken a big bite, sonny. Are you certain that you can chew and swallow?"

"I'll have to find out," Spence sighed.

"I wish you luck. I think you'll be needing it."

Cassie rose from her chair, standing next to Spence, as the old man shuffled from the room. Her hand found Spence's.

"I'm frightened for you, Spencer. What if...?"

"Don't you fret, Cassie," he told her confidently. "I've got a trick or two up my sleeve."

"Maybe you could tell me. Then I wouldn't worry so much."

His arm slipped around her. "I kind of like having someone worry over me. It's a new experience."

"Dying would be a new experience, too. I don't want you trying that."

"I'll make a point of avoiding that ordeal. You can trust me, Cassie. Everything will turn out just fine."

She lay her head against his shoulder, but he knew she was not taken in by his soothing words. Opposing Daton Umbridge was not a healthy idea. Nor was trying to close the asylum and put Vanbough behind bars. It was a job that one man wasn't enough for—and both of them knew it. But he couldn't wait for the federal government or the Colorado government to act. That would take ages.

Riley O'Shay didn't look happy about the news of the shooting, but he seemed even more upset about the findings out at the Mattlock spread.

"You've done stirred up a nest of rattlers, Kane. What do you intend on doing with them now?"

"You're the law in Junction City, O'Shay. I think you ought to open an investigation."

"Investigation? Me?" He was incredulous at the thought. "I ain't got no jurisdiction to start an investigation out there. I'm a town marshal."

"Then who handles cases out of town?"

"Supposed to be a territorial marshal in Colorado someplace, but I've never seen him."

"Someone has to take charge, O'Shay. You can't sit by and let people be killed just because they weren't murdered within the limits of your town."

"I sent Baily out with you, and he's the one who ended up being shot. Now you want me to ride out and tell Daton that we're going to snoop around for evidence that might convict him of murder. What kind of fool do you take me for, Kane?"

"I take you for an honest man. I take you for a marshal, a man who sees his duty and will do it."

"Your crystal ball is a little cloudy, son. I don't see myself doing any such thing."

"What do you suggest then? Certainly someone looked into the murder of Steel and Mattlock. Who handled that?"

O'Shay paced his office, hands locked behind his back. He wore a star, but locking up a drunk on a Saturday night was about the extent of his law enforcement.

"Have you talked to Judge Clott on this?"

"He isn't an investigator either. He is the one who is supposed to listen to evidence— after it gets to a courtroom."

"In other words, he told you to go soak your head."

"Something like that."

The marshal shook his head in wonder. "I've got to admire you for your gall, Kane. You get a letter of approval from the governor saying you can inspect the asylum, and you end up trying to start an investigation of three murders. I might add that none of those murders is relevant to your inspecting the asylum."

"I'm not a single-minded lawyer, O'Shay. When I cross an injustice, I like to see it rectified. I was kind of hoping that you were that kind of lawman."

"Between us, we don't have the authority to step onto Daton Umbridge's ranch, Kane. Yet you expect me to run an investigation on Alvin Peek and the Steel-Mattlock murders. Combine that with the fact that I don't have the slightest idea about how to investigate a murder, and you would have to admit we're in a river without a boat."

"I've an idea or two on that."

The marshal allowed himself a tight grin. "Then I hereby deputize you, Spencer Kane."

"What?"

"You are now a deputy marshal for the fine town of Junction City, Colorado. I appoint you as my personal investigator from this office."

"I can't be a deputy!"

"And why not?"

"Because I'm already serving in an official capacity. I'm—"

"During times of need, I've deputized the judge himself, Kane. You have all of the authority that this office has behind it. If you get yourself killed, I'll have it so read on your marker."

"What about you?"

"When you get enough evidence to convict someone, I'll get up a posse to help you arrest the guilty party."

"That's just great," Spence said dryly. "I now have as much authority as you, and your jurisdiction ends at the town limits."

"That's about the size of it." The marshal grinned. "I'll get you a badge. I've got some in my desk drawer. Got to be official about this, you know."

"Of course, Marshal. I wouldn't want to wear a badge under false pretenses."

O'Shay pinned a tarnished badge on Spence's chest. Then he stood back and grinned at his handiwork. "That'll give Sparks a good target to shoot at."

"Where am I supposed to start this investigation?"

"You said that you had a couple ideas," O'Shay reminded him. "I told you that I didn't know anything about looking into a murder. You just be keeping me informed of your progress."

CHAPTER EIGHTEEN

Laura Woods had a room at a local boardinghouse. As chance would have it, it was the same boardinghouse where Strummer lived.

Watching the house from across the street, Spence waited until several people had left it—one of them being Strummer. He had beaten the man with his fists once, but it never paid to push one's luck. Once the man was gone, headed toward the livery stable, Spence made his way to the front of the building.

He entered to find a woman sweeping the floor. She was gray with years but had a rather kindly face and soft, motherly eyes.

"May I help you, young man?"

"I'm looking for Laura Woods."

"She left just a few minutes ago," the woman replied. "I'm Mrs. Blaine. Can I be of help?"

He looked at her closely. "You are Dr. Blaine's wife?"

She smiled. "If you choose to look at it that way. You might also think that Dr. Blaine is my husband."

He smiled at her joke. "I didn't know the two of you ran a boardinghouse."

"Being a doctor doesn't have monetary rewards out West, young man. We couldn't live off what little he earned. Too many people put him off or paid with a chicken or eggs or a pig. We had to do something to keep a roof over our heads."

"I can believe that."

"What did you need to see Laura about? Perhaps I could help you find her."

"I'm afraid I was only doing some snooping, ma'am. She isn't all that eager to meet me, I'm sure of that."

"Ah, yes." The woman's eyes shone. "You're that dude, the lawyer who's stirring up things at the asylum."

"That's correct."

"I could tell you a few things about that place," she said, her face growing more serious. "That quack, Dr. Vanbough, and his staff—what a bunch of butchers they are!"

"I wasn't aware that many people were informed of the treatment the inmates were getting."

"My husband is called on to treat some of the poor creatures on occasion. He's told me plenty about that place!"

"Really?" Spence felt his pulse begin to race. "Your husband and I didn't get much chance to talk. Perhaps you and I could discuss a few things about that madhouse."

"Maybe even about Laura?" The woman's eyes narrowed. She was old in years, but she had a sharp mind.

"If it would help shed light on Gloria Umbridge's death," Spence said.

"Seeing how that woman pays her rent in advance now, and knowing she quit her job a couple months back, I might be able to tell you more than you care to know."

"You'll find that I'm a willing listener, Mrs. Blaine. You must know what I'm up against here, so any help you can give me would be a blessing."

"Let's sit and have some coffee," she suggested. "This might take a bit of time."

Sparks signaled to Seeton, and the man moved the wagon and team into place at the rear of the store.

"Hold them here!" Sparks whispered. "I'll get the girl."

"What if you are seen?" Seeton wanted to know, his eyes searching the back street for any people.

"Bob is still laid up in bed. That means his wife is in the store. I'll bring Cassie out the back way."

Seeton continued to look around nervously. "Well, get with it then, Sparks. I don't like this one bit. Kidnapping could get us both killed!"

Slipping silently into the rear of the Baily house, Sparks wished that Strummer had been the man Vanbough had sent with him. This man, Seeton, was tough and rough with inmates, but he was basically a coward.

The sound of a woman softly humming led Sparks to Cassie. She had her back to him, washing up the morning dishes. By the time she realized that someone had entered the kitchen, he was within reach. He struck her squarely under the chin before she could cry out. The blow dazed her, and only a soft moan escaped her lips. Then she was over his shoulder, and Sparks was hurrying out to the wagon.

Seeton held up a tarp, but Sparks was taking no chances with the girl. He bound and gagged her quickly, before allowing Seeton to cover her with the tarp.

"You know what to do," Sparks said.

"I'm on my way," Seeton answered. "If that nosy lawyer shows up, there won't be any sign of Cassie."

"Get going then."

Seeton didn't have to be told twice. He flipped the reins lightly, slapping the team of horses into motion. Sparks watched him until the man was out of sight. Then he was hurrying to his own horse.

He smiled, pleased with himself. He'd pulled it off. Let the lawyer figure his way out of this one! If Kane didn't drop his investigation now, he'd never see Cassie again. Her hearing was coming up, and she wouldn't be around to attend. There was no sign of a struggle at Baily's place, so it could easily be maintained that she simply ran off. That would be enough to convince a judge to put her away once more. She'd never show her face in the town of Junction City again.

Sparks didn't kid himself. Spencer Kane would not give up his case so easily. That really didn't matter, for all that was required at the moment was his resignation from the investigation he'd undertaken. Once he agreed to that, there could be a nasty accident. Spencer had to be killed, and Sparks was just the man to oversee the job.

There might be a few suspicions after that, but it would all quiet down after a spell. Cassie would either rot at the asylum, or she would end up like Gloria. It wasn't pleasant to think of, for Cassie had never hurt a soul. She was pretty, a real lady, and innocent of any wrongdoing.

Sighing deeply, Sparks shrugged the girl out of his mind. It was his job to keep Daton on top of the entire valley. If Cassie Mattlock was a threat to that, she would have to be taken care of.

Spence rode toward the Umbridge ranch. He needed to get the bill of sale for the Mattlock spread. Cassie had told him that she knew what Alvin's signature looked like, and if he hadn't signed the paper, Spence would have the motive he needed to prove that Daton was behind the death of at least one man.

Spence didn't reach the ranch house. He was intercepted by Daton Umbridge. The man left a crew of several men to ride over and confront Spence.

"You lost, lawyer?"

"Just on my way up to see you, Daton."

"That right?"

"I want to pick up the bill of sale for the Mattlock spread. I'll need it for Cassie's hearing."

"What for?"

"It's relevant to her defence. You certainly don't need the girl behind those walls anymore. After all, you have the ranch, and it's all legal."

Daton leaned forward in the saddle, searching Spence's poker face.

"You ain't fooling me one bit, Kane. You're up to something—I can feel it."

"I'm only trying to get Cassie released from the asylum."

"That why you're wearing a deputy marshal badge?"

Spence lifted a careless shoulder. "The marshal thought you might be more willing to cooperate if I looked like I was acting in a more official capacity."

"I don't believe a word of what you've said, Kane," Daton grunted in contempt. "What's your real game?"

"You're not a trusting sort, are you?"

"I know that you've been snooping around, digging up bodies and the like. I figure your stakes are not just getting Cassie freed from the asylum."

Spence sighed his resignation. Daton was no fool. He knew what was really at stake.

"I'm looking into the murder of Alvin Peek, Daton. You might not be surprised one bit that you are a prime suspect."

Daton laughed. "And you want me to hand over the papers to the Mattlock place? Then you go find someone who'll testify that the signature isn't Alvin's. That would point a finger right at me for his death, wouldn't it?"

"You're already implicated. It was your hired man who tried to kill Bob Baily and myself."

"You were trespassing."

"He gave no warning, nor did he even question us. The man was intent upon killing us both, and he had no justification for that."

"That don't prove that I knew anything about it," Daton said.

"Then there's other matters to consider in this case."

"Such as?" the rancher asked.

"The deaths of Jerrod Steel and Joe Mattlock."

"Probably killed by Alvin for the inheritance," Daton said easily.

"And there's the confinement of Cassie and Gloria into the asylum. Evidence might turn up to show that they were put into that place without justification. That would make Vanbough an accomplice to anything you had up your sleeve. I wonder if he has the backbone to stand up to a murder charge."

Daton's face darkened now. His patience was gone, for he was used to having other men bend and bow in front of him. He was not accustomed to being challenged.

"I think you'd better ride off of my property, Kane. Your health might be in real jeopardy here."

"I can summon that bill of sale in court, Daton."

"Then you'll have to do just that. I want you off of my place, and I want you off right now!"

Spence held his ground for a long moment, meeting the hostile glare of the powerful ranch owner. Then he turned his horse back toward town. He couldn't defeat a man like Daton in a head-on confrontation. He would have to work behind the man's back, to undermine his strength, to strike at his weaknesses—providing he even had a weakness.

He kicked the horse into a lope. A meal with Cassie would give him renewed strength. Then he would seek out Sonny or Aaron. Perhaps he could get the information he wanted from them. They might not be so protective of Daton, once all the facts came to light.

CHAPTER NINETEEN

Cassie felt the throbbing in her head, then the chill of the damp air around her. She blinked at the stabbing pain that seemed to blind her and worked her jaw slowly, tenderly. Then she vainly tried to stretch her legs—and realized she was in one of the cages at the asylum again.

"No!" she cried. "Let me out!"

But no one heard her.

"Spence!" she wailed, knowing how stupid it was to call to a man who could not possibly be within miles of the place. "Spence! Help me!"

Something scurried past her feet and she shrieked in alarm. It was a rat, a big one.

Cassie searched for the single blanket that was thrown into each cage. It was dirty, matted with straw and mud, but she brushed at it as best she could to make it usable.

"Cold!" a tiny voice whispered from the cage next to Cassie's. "I'm cold!"

Searching in the near-total darkness, Cassie could barely make out a slender figure a few feet away.

"Jenny?"

"I cold," the girl repeated in her thin voice.

Cassie's heart went out to the simple-minded child. She could make her out in the grayness, sitting with her knees drawn together, her arms wrapped around them. She was rocking back and forth, as if consoling herself.

"It'll be all right, Jenny," Cassie told the girl. "Help will soon come."

The girl stopped rocking, looking closely at Cassie. "I—I'm cold," she repeated.

"I'd throw you my blanket, but the mesh around the bars won't let me get it out of the cage."

The little girl went back to the rocking motion once more. She looked very sad, very alone, very forlorn.

As Cassie watched Jenny, she wondered how she had been snatched away from the

Baily house. What had happened to Spence?

She feared he might be fighting for his life at that very moment. How else would they dare kidnap her right out of a house? Daton must have planned something very big, and that could only mean trouble for both her and Spence Kane.

Cassie blinked back her tears. She would have to be strong and patient. She would wait for Spence to come save her. After all, she had no other choice. But what if he didn't come?

Riley was nearing the Baily store when Spence rode back to town. He didn't like the look on the lawyer's face. He didn't like it one bit.

"Light down, Kane," O'Shay greeted him. "We've got more trouble in the pot."

Spence climbed down from his horse and waited for the marshal to continue. As they both entered the store, he observed that Emma looked very worried.

"Let's have it," he prodded the marshal.

"Cassie is gone."

"Gone where?"

"We don't know," the marshal sighed, shaking his head sadly. "According to Mrs. Baily, she was doing the dishes one minute and gone the next. There is no sign of a struggle and nothing is missing from the house."

"I think I detect the odor of Daton Umbridge and Dr. Vanbough," Spence declared. "They've kidnapped her!"

"That's a serious charge, son," O'Shay said. "Maybe the girl had someplace to go. There's a chance that someone came and got her for some reason—other than foul play."

"No one knew she was staying here, Marshal," Spence told the lawman.

"What do you aim to do then?"

Spence looked at the marshal. The lawman was as helpless as a child, looking to a city lawyer to tell him how to do his job. He should have been taking charge, organizing a search—but, no. He was only a puppet with a badge.

"Get over to Judge Clott's place, O'Shay," Spence said, taking the reins in his own hands. "I want a warrant to search both the asylum and Daton's ranch."

"There's twenty cabins and shacks on Daton's place! How can we possibly search them all?"

"One at a time," Spence told him. "But first, I'll ride out and have a few words with Daton's sons. I've picked up a little information that they might be interested in."

"You think you can get them to side us against their own father?"

"I'm not taking anything for granted, O'Shay, but I'll tell you one thing for certain." Spence clenched his teeth. "I aim to find Cassie, and heaven help the man who touches or harms her in any way!"

The marshal seemed taken aback by the cold steel in Spence's voice.

"I'll get those orders. You can count on that."

Spence nodded. Then he went out and mounted his horse.

With the help of a farmer, who gave him directions, Spence neared the coal mine an hour later. At one side, he spotted several wagons. As luck would have it, Sonny was examing one of the wagons. He walked over to meet Spence, neither hostility nor friendship visible in his eyes.

"Howdy, lawyer," he said evenly. "What brings you way up here?"

Spence stopped his horse. "I'd like to talk to you and Aaron about your mother."

"We had it out with our pa already. He says that you're just trying to turn us against him."

"Only if that is what he deserves, Sonny," Spence maintained. "Only if he did your mother a great injustice and is responsible for her death."

"Aaron is riding over this afternoon," Sonny said slowly. "He ought to be here at any time. We were going to take some coal into town, but one of the wagons is over at the ranch."

"Isn't that where it belongs?" Spence asked with interest.

"It wasn't there yesterday. Sparks had taken it into town for some supplies. I don't see that the wagon is all that important."

"I didn't think Sparks was the kind of man who ever did any manual labor. I kind of figured someone else would gather the grub and supplies for the ranch."

"Usually that's so. I don't know why Sparks volunteered this time." Sonny's eyes narrowed. "You wouldn't be fishing for something, would you?"

"Cassie was kidnapped from the Baily house this morning. I thought that a wagon might have hidden her, while whoever bagged her got out of town."

"Light down, Kane," Sonny said. "Let's wait until Aaron gets here. You start talking kidnapping, you're talking a hanging for someone. Maybe Aaron has heard something that's in the wind."

CHAPTER TWENTY

Aaron was silent, listening to Spence. Sonny looked mostly at his older brother, as if wondering how the news was affecting him. Spence wasn't painting a pretty picture.

"You claim that our pa has been paying for Laura Woods's board and keep?" Aaron said.

"According to Mrs. Blaine. The doctor's wife told me that Laura has plenty of spending money right now. Seems she quit her job a short time after your mother was put into the Country Acre Asylum."

The two boys exchanged glances.

"Cassie says there wasn't anything wrong with your mother. I think Gloria was simply

161

in the way of a budding romance—one between Daton and Laura."

Aaron paced about, his fists clenched.
There was anger on his face, hurt in his eyes.

"Blast you, Spencer Kane!" he snarled.
"You expect us to take your word against our
own father! What kind of man are you?"

"The kind that insists on justice. Alvin was
buried on his own place. He never left the
country with any money. I believe that Steel
and Joe Mattlock were killed in cold blood."

"Aaron?" Sonny asked his brother. "What
are we going to do? We can't go against our
own pa!"

Aaron had tears in his eyes. He turned
away from the two of them, trying to regain
his composure.

"I reckon we've been lazy at times," Sonny
said. "I guess we got into trouble on occasion,
on account of being wild. Though we didn't
hurt anyone, we used to sometimes raise
hell." He lowered his voice. "Only, Ma never
even had a harsh word for us. She used to
say, 'Make me proud, sons. I know you're
good boys.' And we—we didn't even go to see
her in that rotten, stinking hole!"

Aaron spun on him. "Pa said not to! Vanbough and Pa both kept us away!"

"The reason for that ought to be obvious,"
Spence put in. "If you'd have seen your

mother, you'd have demanded that she be returned home. She would have once again been in the way of Daton and Laura."

Sonny looked squarely up at Spence. "Sparks and Mutt killed Jerrod Steel and Joe Mattlock. I heard them talking about it."

"What about Alvin?" Spence asked.

"Everyone thought he left the country. Pa drew out the money from the bank and rode out to pay him. The last we heard, Alvin took the cash and disappeared."

"Did your father go out to the Mattlock spread alone?"

"No," Aaron said. "Sparks went with him." His face took on a sour look. "He was to safeguard the money."

"Where do you think they would take Cassie?" Spence said, getting back to the problem at hand.

"They wouldn't take her to the ranch, for there ain't a regular hand on the payroll who would hold with kidnapping," Aaron surmised.

"That means she's probably back at the asylum," Sonny deduced.

"I'd guess that as well," Aaron said.

"Then that's where I'll be heading," Spence told them.

"Well, you hold tight for a minute," Aaron said. "We're going with you. I've a question or two that Vanbough can answer for me."

"Right!" Sonny agreed. "Even if Cassie isn't there, we'll ask him a few questions about our mother. I think the guesswork is gone now. We know damn well that she should have never been buried in that pest hole!"

Riley O'Shay had the papers Spence had asked for. The marshal was grim and surprised at seeing the Umbridge boys.

"We're heading over to the asylum, O'Shay. You want to come along?" Spence said.

"I've got the warrants," the marshal answered. "You boys look like you might be heading for some trouble, so I'd best tag along."

"Gather up your horse," Spence told him. "You can catch up with us."

Riley came thundering up on the three of them a mile short of the asylum gate. He looked full of excitement, his hat tightly seated on his head, his gun tied on his hip. Spence was somewhat surprised to see that he was game for this encounter.

"Strummer is on the gate," Sonny noticed from afar. "How'll we handle this?"

"Just like a freight train," Spence told him. "We plow through everything in our way. If it doesn't move, we run over it."

"He's your meat," Aaron said. "You proved that you could take him once."

"Let's hope he has a little more respect for the law that's riding with us. I don't feel like wasting myself in another brawl."

Strummer stood poised at the gate, his hands on his hips, but for some reason, he appeared cautious and a bit uncertain.

"Open up," Spence told him. "We have a warrant to search the grounds."

Strummer looked at the badge on Spence's chest, then at the three other riders.

"What kind of visit is this?"

"A formal one. Now open the gate."

Strummer reluctantly unlocked the gate, then swung it open to allow the four men onto the grounds. Once they were inside, he closed and locked the steel gate behind them. Spence didn't have to look back to know the man was following them.

Vanbough came out to the porch, awaiting the four of them. He didn't look disturbed in the slightest.

"Well, Marshal ... Aaron ... Sonny, this is a real surprise. What brings you here today?"

"I've a search warrant," Riley informed the steel-eyed doctor. "We intend to have a good look around."

"Certainly," the man smiled. "Perhaps I could help. What are we looking for?"

"Cassie Mattlock."

"But, Marshal," the man said innocently, "don't you remember? Cassie was recently released from here."

Spence was already walking past the man. He knew his way into the wards. As he went, he pushed open every door and looked into each room.

The marshal was content to follow, as were both Aaron and Sonny. They weren't ready to confront Vanbough just yet. He would be easier to rattle once they had something on him.

The women's ward held only five women. Spence questioned the witch, but she refused to answer him. The men were the same, still eleven in the room, and even the one trying to bark like a dog again.

Inside the children's ward, he spotted Jenny. She was sitting in a corner of the room, a blanket wrapped around her shoulders. She looked very sad and very tired.

Sonny and Aaron had split off to examine the outside and other rooms. Even the marshal had done some searching on his own. All of them returned with the same results. No one had seen or heard Cassie. She was nowhere to be found.

"I told you," Vanbough grinned, joining

them all in the children's ward. "Cassie isn't here."

It was only by accident that Spence noticed Jenny's head snap up at the mention of Cassie's name. He crossed the room to kneel down next to her.

"Hello, Jenny," he said softly. "How are you?"

"Bad girl," she whispered. "Jenny bad girl."

"No," he said cradling her face with tender hands. "Jenny is a good girl. Jenny is a pretty girl."

The child's eyes were large and brown. She looked at Spence with awe.

"Do you remember Cassie?" he asked.

"C-Cassie," she said.

"Yes. Have you seen Cassie? Can you tell me where she is?"

The girl's head bobbed up and down.

"Show me, Jenny," he coaxed. "Where is Cassie?"

"The child has the mind of a two-year-old!" Vanbough cried. "Are you crazy yourself, Kane?"

"Even two-year-olds have memories and brains, Vanbough. You just stay out of our way."

The doctor might have protested, but

Aaron grabbed him by the scruff of the neck and jerked him out of the room. The others stood back, not blocking Jenny's way.

"Show me where Cassie is, Jenny," Spence prompted the child again. "Take me to her."

Jenny clung to her blanket, but she got to her feet. Then she walked stiffly out of the room. She stopped in the hallway, as if afraid to go on. Spence took hold of her hand and smiled at her.

"No one is going to hurt you, Jenny. Help me find Cassie."

She led him slowly down the corridor. When she reached a door that led outside, she stopped.

"Where do we go now?"

The girl looked up at Spence, then pointed at the floor. "C-cold," she said.

"The floor is cold?"

Jenny shook her head and pointed at the floor. "C-Cassie."

Then Spencer saw the latch against the wall. The floor had been laid evenly, with all of the cracks running the same way. It hid the opening of a trap door. Jenny stepped to one side as he pulled the wooden door upward. Then he was going down the ladder, dropping onto the dirt floor of the cage area.

Cassie was shivering from the cold. Her clothes were damp and covered with dirt, but she came out of the cage with a cry of joy, after the key had been obtained from the doctor. Spence took her into his arms and held her for a long time.

"I prayed to God that you'd find me before nightfall," she whispered when they were upstairs again. "I was so frightened that they'd done something to you."

"They've done it to themselves this time. Who brought you here?"

"They were all in on it," she answered. "Strummer, Seeton, Vanbough, and Sparks. Sparks said that Daton wanted me out of the way, that they were going to force you to stop your investigation."

"It might have worked, had they ever caught up with me. I was so busy scouring the countryside, they never had a chance to even make me the offer."

"What now?"

"Now we close up this place. I don't want anyone to ever have to come down into this hole again."

"I'm with you."

Aaron had a strangle hold on Vanbough, but Sonny and Riley were pulling him off.

Spence glanced at the doctor. "Accessory to murder, to kidnapping, illegally confining patients. Not to mention the horrible treatment of your inmates here. I think I see a long sentence coming for you, Vanbough."

"No! You can't do that to me!"

"Start talking, butcher!" Aaron snarled. "Or I'll bury you in one of your own underground cages!"

"I only...I mean..."

"Perhaps a stay in one of your cages would do your tongue some good," Spence said. "Put him in the hole."

Sonny and Aaron grabbed the man's arms. He cried out, struggling against them. At the same time, Strummer lumbered inside the building.

Spence asked him, "You want to try your luck a second time?"

"Seeton rode off to warn Daton and Sparks," Strummer said with a sly grin. "I wonder if you'll be so tough against a hundred riders!"

"Wait!" Vanbough cried, being forced toward the ladder. "I'll talk! Don't put me in a cage. I wouldn't live through the night. I'm not a well man!"

"Then talk!" Aaron snapped, holding the man by his hair. "Lie to me once, and I'll twist your rotten head off!"

Spence waited, touched by the way Jenny slipped up against Cassie. He knew what Vanbough would say. There was little doubt that Gloria Umbridge had been put away to get rid of her. As for Cassie, he knew she'd been put away for the same reason. Daton had almost everything work for him. If the Bailys had not written to the governor, the entire plan would have worked.

CHAPTER TWENTY-ONE

It didn't take long to lock Strummer and Vanbough away. Right afterward, Riley had a talk with the banker. Then Daton had to be dealt with. There would be no posse, for a large body of men might have instigated a real war. Instead, Bob Baily took charge of the prisoners. For he was now able to sit and guard them. That left Riley, Spence, and the two Umbridge boys to confront Daton and his many men.

Cassie, meanwhile, took charge of the asylum, with Emma Baily coming out to pitch in. Three of the young men in town also came out to handle any hard labor or trouble from the inmates. All the former guards had been dismissed.

"Interesting," Riley told Spence as they rode to the ranch. "Daton borrowed money one day and paid it back the next. I guess that'll put the nail in his coffin over the killing of Alvin Peek. The amount was three thousand dollars. That means the signature is probably Alvin's."

"No need to forge his name when they were intent on killing him from the start," Spence said.

"Sparks killed Jerrod Steel and Joe Mattlock," Sonny added. "I heard them talking it over—him and Mutt. I reckon that makes our pa an accessory to that pair of murders, too."

"You know we'd go this alone, Aaron... Sonny, if we didn't need you to keep the ranch hands out of the fight," Spence said.

Aaron was grim. "All I can think of is our ma, suffering in that dirty, filthy place. We let her die like some kind of animal, and it was Daton who put her there. I never figured Pa could be so cold-blooded."

"Let's hope Daton is confident enough to stand trial. I'd hate to get us all killed," Spence said.

"Ditto for that," Riley grunted. "I'm too young to die."

* * *

"Stand fast!" Sparks growled at Seeton. "You ain't got the guts of a gnat!"

"I only come to warn you," Seeton cried. "I ain't waiting for a posse to come riding in here to drag us all off to jail!"

"You'll stick here with us," Sparks warned the man.

"The boys will be in from the pastures pretty quick," Daton said. "Spence Kane isn't going to get much of a posse up against my ranch."

"He had your sons with him!" Seeton said. "I tell you, we'll all end up hanging from the gallows!"

"Settle down!" Daton snapped.

"I'm getting out of here!" Seeton wailed, charging out of the house to grab up the reins of his horse.

"Hold it!" Sparks shouted.

But Seeton was scared. He swung onto the back of his horse and jerked him around. That was about the time a gun roared. The bullet dusted the front of Seeton's chest, a tiny hole visible through his shirt. He was dead before he felt the ground beneath his body.

"You didn't have to shoot him," Daton complained.

"He'd have sung his head off to save himself, boss. The lawyer don't have proof of nothing. If he had that coward singing for him, he'd put us away for good."

Daton looked down at the body, then up at several approaching riders. "Put his gun in his hand. Make it look like it was a fair fight."

Sparks hurried to follow orders, barely getting back to the porch before Kane and the others rode into the yard.

Spence stopped next to the body and looked down. "Trouble, Umbridge?"

"The man tried to blackmail me for money," Daton said easily. "He said he'd testify that Gloria didn't need to be put into the asylum. He demanded cash. When I wouldn't give him a dime, he tried to kill me. Sparks here got him first."

"I don't believe a word of that," Spence told the rancher. "Seeton was basically yellow. I don't see him drawing against Sparks or you."

A group of riders came into the yard from behind the house. There were fifteen or more of them, all carrying guns. Before the dust settled from their horses, there was a second bunch.

Spence and Riley faced about thirty armed men. It would have been a suicide encounter, except for Aaron and Sonny. They moved up next to the two lawmen.

"Pa is under arrest," Aaron said solemnly. "There are some matters that have to be cleared up in court."

"Son!" Daton exclaimed. "You can't mean that!"

But Sonny was nodding at his brother's side. "You put away our mother, Pa. You killed her, as sure as if you'd put a gun to her head."

"You're wrong!"

"We know about Laura Woods," Aaron replied. "We know who's paying her bills. Your trips into town haven't gone unnoticed."

"As for you, Sparks," Riley told the gunman, "we have a witness who can testify that you killed Jerrod Steel and Joe Mattlock. Put your guns down and come along peacefully."

Sparks looked at Daton. "We can take them, boss. We've got no choice!"

"I can't kill my own sons!"

"Well, I can!"

Spark's gun was out instantly, but Daton tried to wrestle it away from him. When it discharged, he buckled at the knees.

As Daton fell, mortally wounded, Sparks tried to bring his gun to bear on the four riders in the yard. He was much too slow— thanks to Daton. Aaron and Riley both fired, with Spence also getting off a single shot at the man. Sparks was struck twice, knocked right off the porch.

The riders for the Umbridge ranch merely watched, waiting for the outcome. Then one of them climbed down from his horse to examine Sparks. He shook his head.

"Reckon he won't kill no one else."

Aaron and Sonny went to their father. He was breathing in ragged gasps, his life nearly at an end. He put pain-beclouded eyes on his boys and rocked his head slightly back and forth.

"I—I'm sorry, sons," he grunted. "I—I didn't...didn't mean for...for your ma to die. J-just wanted...wanted..."

"We know," Aaron said quietly.

"Don't hate...."

"We don't hate you, Daton. You're still our pa."

It was hard to tell if the man heard the words or not, for he opened his eyes very wide, then let out a long sigh—a sigh of death.

Driving a wagon was something new to Spence, but it wasn't all that different from a buckboard or carriage. The team consisted of four horses instead of two, but that was all right.

"Are you sure you want to give up your practice?" Cassie asked.

"I'm not giving up my practice," Spence replied. "I'll handle the cases over here in Junction City. We'll kind of ranch in the spare time."

"Ranching is full-time work," Cassie corrected him.

"Aaron has offered to help. I think he'll make us a fine neighbor. It'll be work, but what's success without work?"

Cassie looked over her shoulder at Jenny. The girl was excited at seeing so much of the world, pointing at everything along the way, trying to use her limited vocabulary to describe the fascination she discovered.

"Quite a family you inherited, Spence— husband and father all at once."

He smiled, feeling just fine. "The rewards of winning a case far exceeded my wildest expectations. I think we'll do grand as a family."

Cassie didn't reply to that, scooting over to be a bit closer, resting her hand on his arm. That was the natural way of things, and Spencer couldn't have asked for more out of life. They were a family now, and they'd get by just fine.